Dark Fury

. . . . And the stallion, one of the few remaining great horses of the west, sensing that the frost of age was taking toll of his limbs, felt the desire to make one further foray in the Lost River Valley. He quitted the secret canyon by way of the hidden underground trail, and raiding a ranch in the plains, brought one, Firefly, to his hide-out under Grouse Creek Mountain. This Firefly was, by nature and breeding, a saddle mare, and after a brief sojourn in the canyon, broke away from the herd and trekked back to her home range where, in the fullness of time, she brought forth her foal who was named DARK FURY by reason of his jet black colouring and unbridled character. . . . Dark Fury is the last of the great wild stallions. . . .

(From the Legend of Lost River Valley often mentioned in the Campfire Tales told by Colorado Ted of the Bitter Root Range.)

Joseph E. Chipperfield is well-known for the many books he has written about animals and the American West, including *Ghost Horse*, also published in Beavers.

DARK FURY

Stallion of Lost River Valley

Joseph E. Chipperfield

Beaver Books

First published in 1956 by
Hutchinson Publishing Group Limited
3 Fitzroy Square, London W1P 6JD

This paperback edition published in 1977 by
The Hamlyn Publishing Group Limited
London · New York · Sydney · Toronto
Astronaut House, Feltham, Middlesex, England

ISBN 0 600 32952 6

Printed in England by Cox & Wyman Limited
London, Reading and Fakenham
Set in Intertype Baskerville

For
Phyllis and Ivor Hunt
and their children
Valerie, Vernon and Derrick

Acknowledgements

I would like to acknowledge my thanks for information and assistance accorded to me by The Foreign Service of the United States of America, and Miss Margaret Haferd, the Librarian, at the American Embassy, London.

Also my thanks are due to Mr. Howard C. Lee of the United States Department of Agriculture, (Forest Service), Hamilton, Montana, for information and maps on the Bitter-root Mountain area which is part of the Bitter-root National Forest; to the Forest Supervisors of Challis National Park, Idaho, and Salmon National Forest, Idaho. Last, but not least of those who have been of assistance to me are the Wyoming Travel Commission, Cheyenne, Wyoming, and the Regional Forester, United States Forest Service, Ogden, Utah.

Joseph E. Chipperfield

Contents

Book One
Renegade Stallion

Chapter One

Night coming to the great salt lake desert of Utah was little more than a strange gathering of lilac shadows that only deepened when the last smouldering glow of the sunset flickered and burnt out beyond the ravines and mountains of Nevada. Then no more did the velvet sky contain the etching of mountains brooding afar off. The darkness had taken full possession of the desert, and there was nothing but the emptiness of space with the stars like lanterns gleaming fitfully above.

There was a deep silence too, habitual to the barren land, broken only where a thin, wandering breeze moved amongst the grey-green sage. No nightbird called; no coyote yapped.

The great salt desert stretched in endless waves to where the night stood deepest and intangible, and where only the acrid red-water lakes held vague reflections of the stars.

There was nothing intangible, however, about the small township built on the western edge of the desert, nor yet about the large tent and the chuck wagons that stood on the scrubland adjacent to the dingy main street.

A few glimmering lamps illuminated the scattered shacks, with another dozen or more flickering through the windows of what appeared to be shacks set up on wheels, these latter practically encircling the huge tent. There were a few barred cages close beside the tent in which animals, held captive, peered balefully into the darkness outside, or slept uneasily with heads resting on long-taloned feet.

Tom Burke's Circus was making one of its periodical visits to the Mormon township!

There was an important addition to the circus property that night. Earlier, a high corral had been hastily erected where the scrubland gave way to sour pasture. Inside it, at the end of a long rope secured by a stake driven into the ground, stood a stallion dark as the very night about him. His attitude of nervous tension was indicative of the rage that fired his blood each time he tried to move forward a pace or two, and felt the sharp tug of the rope about his neck.

It was no ordinary stallion for which the corral had been set up at the command of Tom Burke himself. Indeed, no! It was rumoured that the horse was the last of the great wild stallions of the west. Nobody associated with the circus knew much about the animal save what they had been told by the four cowpunchers who had brought him in. Their spokesman, a mean, hard-faced fellow of swarthy appearance, when suggesting to Burke that the horse would make a grand exhibit in the big ring, had merely said that he was called Dark Fury — the name that had been given to him by some Indians of the Cœur D'Alene tribe.

Of the place where the stallion had been found, indeed, even the stallion's very origin, was as much a secret as the origins of the men who had brought him across the dreaded salt desert to become a performer in the small-town circus run by Tom Burke.

Dark Fury himself had no misgivings as to the long journey he had been forced to make by the men who had continually ill-used him from the very moment they had got him at the end of a rope. The only thing he did not remember with any clearness was the manner of his capture. It had happened so quickly, just as the night was ending and he stood drinking from a sink-hole with the wind blowing straight over him.

The men had come up silently, walking into the stiff flow of the wind, and it was not until the stallion felt a lasso settling about his neck that he became aware of the danger that threatened his existence. Even as he reared to fight off the thing that had started to choke him, so did the mean, hard-faced leader who was called Luke by his companions, drive in with a whip which he started to use unmercifully. There was one other with him – a long-legged individual who was not only nimble on his feet, but was equally as sharp with the whip as his partner. In addition, he it was who held on grimly to the rope.

Whilst Dark Fury was still making a firm stand against the assault that was being made on him, two others came riding up. In a trice, the rope was affixed to one of the saddles, and the stallion found himself at a greater disadvantage, for the mustang to which he was now practically tethered was handled by a man expert in bronco breaking.

For a short while, he experienced nothing but pain. The rope tightened about his neck, and constant lashes from the whip brought fire to his limbs. As if to add to his misery, a storm broke over the mountains, and icy rain poured down upon him as he struggled in vain to gain his freedom. . . .

Dark Fury never ceased straining against the rope. Even now, many weeks after his capture, he still struggled against it, recognising it as the symbol of his slavery to man who had now become his master.

On this night as he stood taut with nervous tension in the corral, he was sensing things hidden out there in the darkness. His nostrils flared and repeatedly tested the atmosphere. His peculiar state of tension increased. He could scent strongly those other animals who, like himself, were held captive. In particular, he could scent the mountain lions who were housed in the cage nearest to the corral, and these animals Dark Fury knew as his erstwhile enemies . . . the enemies who had often tyrannised him in that other world he had known so well but a few short months before.

He stood testing the air currents for a long time, listening all the while to the restless sounds of creatures who, like him, were tormented by the dim recollections of happier days.

Dark Fury had no sleep that night. He remained quiet and watchful, the obscurity of the night seeming to envelop him until he and the darkness were one. Then gradually the gloom began to fail and the sky over the desert grew lighter. Dawn was not far off.

With the gathering of light in the east came a sudden trickle of wind, stronger than that which had wandered amongst the sagebrush during the night hours.

The stallion turned and faced the east eagerly, sniffing at the wind and striving to find in it some trace of the far country he knew as home. At first, all Dark Fury could scent was the bitter salty flavour of the desert; then back of the bitter tang a fresher smell with a hint of coldness in it ... the coldness of that northern country which was his home range.

Dark Fury's eyes glowed with a new light; his body tensed as his magnificent head rose slightly the better to receive the flow of the wind that still came in steadily from the north.

In the gathering of the new day, Dark Fury was truly a stallion to command attention. There was not a single trace of colour anywhere amidst his blackness, and from head to foot he possessed all the points of a thoroughbred. His coat shone as the dawn flared in the east. There was no horse to match him in the entire State of Utah, nor in Wyoming or Idaho for that matter. Wild though he might be, he was quite clearly a stallion who had reverted in type to his ancient Arab ancestors.

Then, as the animals in their cages growled to greet the dawn, he swung about, bristling with rage. Truly then was he all his name implied ... a creature of dark fury!

As the light grew stronger, so did the main details of Burke's Circus become revealed. The large tent, referred to by Burke as 'The Big Top' was little better than a huge canvas covering, patched and worn and, in places, badly tattered so that ragged ends fluttered in the breeze. It yet served its purpose, and Burke's Circus was quite a feature of the Middle West, and was always well patronised by the folk who inhabited the various small townships it visited.

Grouped around the tent were the animal cages, not more than a dozen or so, containing mountain lions, some coyotes, a few head of mule deer and a solitary bear, reared in the circus from cubhood. Bruno, as the bear was known, was a good-natured creature, and did not seem to mind being in captivity. Amongst other things, he was the favoured pet of Tom Burke himself, and often in the early morning, was permitted to leave the cage and wander around at the heels of the Irish showman.

Some little distance from the animal cages were the chuck wagons, and quite close to them, the shacks on wheels. These were all gaily painted to resemble the tinker's caravan Tom Burke had known when a youth in his native Ireland.

The entire circus was a travesty of the real thing. Even the huckster's booths set up at the rear of the Big Top were little better than flimsy tents, held together with pieces of rope.

Very garish indeed the scene as every detail became prominently displayed in the sharp morning light. It yet boldly withstood the swift kindling of colours over the eastern desert as the sun came up. Soon, another hot, sultry day began to bring discomfort to the imprisoned animals.

The stallion stood in a position where he could observe the circus tent and chuck wagons. He was waiting for his tormentors to put in an appearance.

Suddenly he heard the bear grunt, then the mountain lions started to move restlessly. A second later, Dark Fury beheld the figure of a young man emerging from one of the caravans, and after a short pause, the fellow began to move in the direction of the corral.

Dark Fury's ears became erect with curiosity. He stood as near to the corral gate as the rope permitted. There was no surge of rage in him now – just that alertness that was the alertness of an animal who sensed with the uncanny instinct of his kind the approach of one he need not fear.

The young fellow, Kirk Merrett, walked with an easy swing. He was anxious to see the stallion. The previous evening when the horse had been brought in by the four cowpunchers, he had been absent from the circus on a mission for Burke. It was quite dark when he had at last ridden into the township, and having been continuously on the move throughout the day, he was dusty and tired. He had spent no more than a few minutes with Burke, acquainting him of the arrangements that had been made with the local storekeeper at Silver Zone Pass on the Nevada border for sufficient supplies to be laid in at the next scheduled stop for the circus. He had then gone to his bunk to sleep soundly until daybreak.

Kirk had known, of course, that someone had already approached Burke about having a stallion as a performer, but since nothing definite had been agreed upon, he knew nothing further until a chance remark from the circus proprietor the previous night had roused his curiosity.

Kirk had, nevertheless, completely forgotten about the horse until he left the caravan next morning and saw the corral.

His face lit up at the sight.

No more than twenty-three years of age, soft-spoken, and lean in appearance with a mass of dark hair, he yet possessed the assurance of one who could well take care of himself in this tough world of even tougher men.

His parents had died when he was ten, and as a result he had spent five years with a grandfather who was more concerned with cattle rustling than in bringing up a lad whose only interest in life seemed to be sitting astride a saddle. In some ways, Kirk's ability to sit straight in a saddle and handle the craziest of mustangs, won the old man's approval. If the old fellow had not met with an untimely end from a sheriff's six shooter, he might have succeeded in making Kirk the best rustler in the Monument Butte country of Wyoming.

As it was, he did succeed in giving Kirk a love of the great open spaces, and after his death the young fellow drifted from place to place, doing an odd job here and there, but for the most part, content to ride from range to range and please himself as to the occupation he followed.

He had been with Tom Burke's Circus for six months – the longest period he had ever stayed in any one job. He was thinking as he walked over to the corral that maybe he had stayed too long with Burke and that it was about time he set off once again on his wanderings.

His brow was a little furrowed at the thought, his very blue eyes, deep set in his head, somewhat grave and thoughtful. Even the tan in his cheeks was heightened a little as he gave serious consideration to the problem.

Then he came to a sudden stop, the question no longer of importance as he stared, open-mouthed, at Dark Fury.

For as long as Kirk could remember, he had regarded a horse as a
creature necessary to carry him from one place to another. Because of
this, he had sought no outstanding attributes in such an animal save
those essential for easy riding, and most of the horses he had ridden
at different times were of the hardy mustang breed. He was always
ready to admit when questioned on their qualities that they were
good horses when once you had mastered them. Even then, they were
inclined to be bad-tempered, and seldom looked other than savage,
ill-kept beasts who would have resented grooming if any attempt
were made to perform such a service.

The stallion in the corral, however, was something altogether
different. Kirk's heart took on a more excited beat as he continued to
stare at Dark Fury who, contrary to all he had heard about so-called
wild horses, seemed quieter than any mustang he had known.

Here, he thought, was no horse that could be run off his feet, but
one who could undoubtedly hold his pace with the best of them and
carry his rider over the sage with a sureness of movement that would
seem like floating on a cloud.

Moreover, such an animal, black as coal, with such a magnificent
head, would be a companion, a creature a man could care for, even
guard jealously. There must be exceptional speed in that great frame
... untold strength in those big, muscular shoulders. . . .

Kirk could not take his eyes off the stallion.

'He's sure some hoss!' he exclaimed involuntarily.

Dark Fury, stretching out his neck and sniffing, gave a short grunt.

Kirk then moved up closer to the corral, his admiration making
him a trifle incautious in his manner of approach.

Suddenly Dark Fury reared, and backed away a few paces. It
seemed to the young fellow that the horse was bent on showing off,
and for one fleeting moment, Kirk thought of the many mountain
retreats he had known in his wanderings, the dark, sunless canyons,
the lush valleys, and for the first time, sensed deep down inside him,
that he would have enjoyed them all so much more had he a horse
like Dark Fury as his companion. Not only that, those nights he had

15

spent in isolation would not have been quite so lonely, and his sleep less uneasy, for the stallion would have been a ready guard ... watching over him with a vigilance that would have outmatched that of a dog.

Kirk came out of his dreaming to the sound of a voice shouting from a way off. Almost immediately, Dark Fury changed to a creature of uncontrollable rage, racing round and round the corral, snorting with hatred.

Luke, the man whom Dark Fury disliked more than any of the others, was approaching.

Kirk was about to saunter off when Luke shouted menacingly; 'You keep away from that hoss, mister. ... He don't like strangers. ...'

To Kirk's surprise, he covered the last few yards at a sharp run. The two men then took stock of each other, the younger man regarding the cowpuncher with a measure of good-humoured curiosity, the other glaring at Kirk with undoubted suspicion.

'Scared the hoss might run away?' Kirk asked at last.

Luke's face reddened at the taunt. He permitted the ungovernable nature of his temper to become revealed in the sudden cording of the veins in his forehead.

'I'm jest warnin' you,' he remarked tensely. 'I don't aim at havin' anybody interferin' with the hoss, or hangin' round the corral. Get me?'

He then attempted to push past Kirk to reach the corral gate.

The younger man stood his ground.

'You'd better quit the shovin', mister,' he said sharply. Then nodding in the direction of Dark Fury, he added: 'Seems to me the hoss don't much care for you either.'

Before Luke could reply, Kirk had turned away.

Just then, the stallion uttered a shrill whistle, and began to paw the ground. The cowpuncher immediately turned his attention to the necessity of getting the horse under control, and still enraged at his encounter with Kirk, entered the corral with a grim purpose in mind.

He proceeded to use the whip on the horse.

There was a rising cry of pain from Dark Fury.

16

Kirk, arrested by the sound, turned and saw what was happening.

A feeling, more powerful than mere anger, swept through him. He straightened up with a jerk. He then raced to Dark Fury's defence unaware that Luke's companions were also approaching.

The sight of the cowpuncher continuing to thrash the stallion lent speed to his feet. . . .

Chapter Two

Dark Fury was plunging violently and trying in vain to free himself from the rope that restricted his movements. He had no direct knowledge of Kirk suddenly turning and racing back towards the corral, neither had he any awareness of Luke's three companions trying to overtake the young fellow. All the stallion could see in his mounting anger was the dancing figure of his persecutor – that nimble, grotesque shape that kept well out of range of his crashing hooves and used the whip with increased violence so that with every crack, it cut deeply into his flanks.

The stallion's eyes were wild; he whinnied, not with fear but with rage. But for the rope that kept him ranging in a prescribed circle, he would have assuredly succeeded in overwhelming his enemy and pounding him beneath his feet.

Then unexpectedly the man sprang away from the horse, and while the animal was still plunging, the fellow ran towards the corral gate which Kirk was trying to open.

In that same instant, the three cowpunchers, having at last reached Kirk, closed in on him. The stallion, still snorting with rage, was himself arrested by a sharp cry this time from the young lad who was gripped savagely from the rear and half-lifted off his feet.

Dark Fury stood taut, staring in the direction of the new conflict that had broken out. Once again his eyes blazed and his ears lay aslant his skull. Even when but a few short seconds before he had no conscious knowledge of Kirk hastening to the corral, so now did he possess no clearly defined reaction to go to the lad's assistance. He merely understood that the men he hated were now attacking some-body else. The fact that it was Kirk possessed no great significance until an association brought about by the sharp note in the lad's voice reminded him of the only kindness he had known since his capture.

He then reared more savagely than ever, trying over and over again to break the fateful hold the rope had on him. His head turned from left to right. He essayed short runs forward; but all to no avail. The rope would not yield. He was only throttling himself in his mad efforts to escape and join the conflict.

Meanwhile, Kirk was being seriously manhandled. Gripped as he was from the rear with his arms pinioned to his sides, there was nothing he could do to defend himself. The three men who had attacked him were as malevolent as their leader. He heard dimly the sound of the corral gate being slammed into place, and far away in the background of noises, the shrill screaming of the stallion. The next moment, a clenched fist brought the salt taste of blood to his lips.

He then heard Luke shouting, and seeing the leer of his face within an inch or so of his own, realised that it was he who had hit him.

'Didn't I tell you to keep away from the corral?'

Luke gave further vent to his feelings by striking Kirk once more, this time with the back of his hand.

'Lay off,' one of his companions said hurriedly. 'Here comes ole man Burke.'

Tom Burke was indeed heading towards the corral, moving as fast as his ungainly legs would allow. A man well past fifty, grizzled with living too long in a hard, dry climate that ill-suited his nature, and with a heavy jowl that quivered as he walked, he was yet a typical showman – a trifle gaudy in dress and possessing a tie-pin that sparkled in his cravat with the falseness of glass.

As he approached the still struggling men, his face was red with indignation. Having no kith and kin of his own, he had taken a special liking to Kirk Merrett and had no wish to see him injured.

'What's goin' on?' he bellowed as he came to a halt, puffing with the exertion he had made in crossing the showground at an unaccustomed pace.

Kirk found himself released, and he immediately swung around to retaliate on those who had taken such an unfair advantage of him.

'Hold yeer hosses, Kirk,' Tom Burke exclaimed. Then speaking direct to Luke, he asked: 'Why were you beatin' up the lad?'

'We were tryin' to stop him enterin' the corral, Mister Burke. He'd be killed fer sure with the stallion fair bent on showin' his paces.'

He nodded in the direction of Dark Fury who, now that the conflict had ended, had become very quiet, staring puzzled at the men outside the corral.

'Seems you were bent on killin' the boy instead,' Burke replied. Then to Kirk, he said: 'Is it true what he says?'

'It certainly is not,' the lad answered quickly. 'This feller' – indicating Luke – 'was whippin' the hide off the hoss, an' for no reason at all that I could see.'

Burke was impressed by the heat in Merrett's tones. He looked to the cowpuncher for a reply to Kirk's accusation.

Luke laughed.

'The lad's too soft. He's never seen anyone handlin' a wild hoss, before. That's why he's all steamed up.'

He tried to hold the showman's piercing glance.

'It's as I said, boss. That hoss is no ordinary crittur. ... He's real wild, an' could be a killer if he ain't kept well under. ...'

'That's a lie, an' you know it,' Kirk said angrily. 'The hoss was quiet enough when I first saw him. ... Seems he was more like a range stallion than a wild hoss.'

There was a restive movement from Luke's friends at this remark, and Luke himself was about to defend his actions when Burke, who realised that wild or not, the stallion was likely to be a great draw to small-town audiences, took Kirk by the arm.

'Best leave the lad alone in future,' he said slowly to the cowpunchers, 'an' don't let me hear too much about you riggin' that hoss. ... He ain't no good if he goes into the ring scary-eyed an' with whip cuts on his hide. Jest remember that!'

He then proceeded to lead Kirk away, despite the young man's attempts to remain and finish out the argument.

Later that morning, after his morning chores had been carried out, Kirk sat on the steps of his chuck wagon and kept close watch on the corral and its inhabitants.

He had learnt from Burke that Luke's other name was Unwin, and that his comrades were known as Bill Maitland, Tim Corson and Enos Wills. Wills, from all accounts, was the second in command of the quartet, and was the lean, long-legged individual who, like Unwin, was quick in the use of a gun and brutal with a whip.

As Kirk saw it, following their morning encounter with Burke, the cowpunchers were not over anxious in incurring his further displeasure. They seemed to be treating the stallion with more consideration, and on occasions, particularly when they thought Kirk was paying very special attention to what they were doing, they displayed a marked tolerance towards Dark Fury, even when he refused to do as they instructed and pulled obstinately against them.

In spite of his very limited experience of performing animals, Kirk was not long in realising that the men's claim to have a show horse was only true in one respect, and that was in the matter of appearance. In all else, the stallion was as undisciplined a creature as he had ever seen in his life before.

After what seemed a long period of activity in the corral it was midday, and Dark Fury's training came to an end and the stallion was left to brood once again upon the indignities that had been heaped upon him.

The long afternoon was slow in passing, the heat intense. While most of the circus folk spent the siesta in their wagons the cowpunchers, to be different, adjourned to the one and only eating house in the town, much to Kirk's relief.

Dark Fury panted as the relentless sun poured its heat upon him. There was no shade anywhere to afford him shelter. The corral was little better than a soured enclosure that threw back glare for glare and where the very stakes glimmered with the heat they attracted. He was also continually worried by the desert flies – huge, buzzing creatures that stung him whenever they managed to get a hold on his hide, and as a result, the stallion was forced to keep on the move in an effort to shake them off.

Almost as bad as the flies was the constant rubbing of the rope about his neck. Each step he took caused the noose to tighten and his resistance to it reminded him of his captivity, thus heightening his misery.

Then he saw Kirk coming towards the corral. Regardless of the warning he had received, and clearly emboldened by the absence of the cowpunchers, the lad carried a bucket of water. It was obvious that he intended entering the corral.

The stallion stood in eager anticipation, his neck arched, and his ears pricked in excitement. No sound did he make as he witnessed the gate swinging open, and no movement came from him as Kirk drew in closer. Then the lad paused, holding out the bucket of water.

Without fear or hesitation, acting almost like a range stallion receiving attention in his home corral, Dark Fury plunged his nose into the water and drank deeply, quite unconcerned that it was Kirk who was holding the bucket.

All the while he drank, the lad was speaking to him in tones intended to allay any fears he might have. The stallion, however, in spite of his general distrust of men, possessed no conscious feeling of antagonism towards Kirk. What restraint there was in him sprang from his usual caution when face to face with something he could not readily classify. Way back in his long life were the stored-up visions of experiences that, though new to him at the time of their happening, had yet been the experiences of those who had been his ancestors; and in those experiences had been men both evil and good. Those who had dealt cruelly with him had not been forgotten. The few that had been kind were, by very reason of their slight impact upon him, little more than an illusive memory hidden deep in the dark mirror of his consciousness.

Notwithstanding, having already sensed that Kirk was kindly disposed towards him, those obscure memories of earlier men with similar characteristics roused a response that was both tolerant and spontaneous. Even as Kirk seemed to possess no fear of him, he was unaware of any sensation of fear himself.

Three times during that tiring afternoon, Kirk visited the corral, always first making sure that the cowpunchers were nowhere visible; and on each occasion, the stallion stood quietly at the end of his rope, waiting for the bucket to be put within reach of his muzzle.

Kirk was a trifle mystified at Dark Fury's easy submission to him, particularly when viewed in relationship to the rage he showed whenever Luke Unwin and his companions were about. Merrett supposed that the answer lay in the fact that the horse resented being handled by men who believed so much in the use of a whip to achieve their purpose.

It was none the less a puzzling business. Merrett felt that he could work wonders with the horse if only he had the opportunity, *and* without any whip to enforce his wishes.

Once more he went off into his day-dreaming, his back resting against the upper step of the chuck wagon, and one leg swinging idly as if in unison with the passing to and fro of his hazy thoughts.

At last the afternoon faded in brightness and colour. Shadows began to gather afar off over the desert, and the distant mountains took on a darker hue as the sun went westering over the ramparts of the canyons of Nevada, and a cool wind came snaking through the small Mormon township, stirring the tattered canvas of the tents of Burke's Circus to bring relief to the suffering animals.

Burke's Circus had already given three performances before Dark Fury became another member of its animal parade. Because the stallion had arrived at the end of the week, and the Mormons permitted no diversions savouring of entertainment during the period of their Sabbath, the horse was not advertised to make an appearance in the ring until the following week. This gave the four men who claimed to own him a little more time to prepare him for his debut.

Hour after hour, first Luke Unwin, then Enos Wills, took on the remorseless routine necessary to make Dark Fury at least presentable. Gradually, they wore down the stallion's resistance, or at least, appeared to do so much to the delight of Bill Maitland and Tim Corson who, always conspicuous in the corral, hooted and shouted after the manner of the audience the horse was expected to please.

On the Monday night, during the evening performance, Tom Burke, with all the swagger of a man about to make a momentous announcement, declared that on the following evening, and for three further evenings in succession, he would present for the entertainment of his audiences the greatest discovery he had yet made. . . .

'None other,' he shouted in his best showman style, 'than the last of the great wild stallions. . . . DARK FURY!'

His voice boomed in the confined space of the so-called Big Top. There was a burst of applause from his motley listeners, and the band, comprising four instruments of brass, all badly played to the accompaniment of a big drum, gave what he considered was a satisfying conclusion to his announcement.

He stood bowing under the flare of the oil lamps, with a few beads of perspiration glistening on his forehead as he finally bowed himself out of the ring, the tie-pin in his cravat seeming less prominent in the insipid yellow light.

Kirk Merrett, standing in his accustomed place in one of the gangways, noted amongst the audience a number of impassive Indians. Most remarkable about them was the sudden look of interest that, for a brief instant, appeared on their faces when Tom Burke mentioned the name 'Dark Fury'.

The young fellow had the distinct feeling that they possessed some knowledge of the stallion. So firm was this sensation in him that he decided to question them immediately the evening performance was over.

Unfortunately, he was late in leaving the arena, and outside, in the half-light made hideous by the flickering flares from the huckster's booths, he had only a dim impression of the Indians moving through the crowd, and making for some mustangs tethered on the outskirts of the showground. Before he could overtake them they were in their saddles and riding away, mere shadows of men bent low over their mounts . . . wise men, perhaps, in that they did not speak one to the other, but rode away into the night as unobtrusively as they had come. . . .

Kirk learnt later that they were of the Cœur D'Alene tribe.

Chapter Three

The Mormon township close to which Burke had set up his circus was a very old place. It had certainly been built to withstand the hot climate which, so often, caused wood to warp and stone to crumble. The dwellings, while being decidedly dingy, were yet in a good state of preservation. There was but the one main street, a dusty thoroughfare, flanked on either side by the stores that served the inhabitants' many requirements. At the west end, in a small square, was the one and only church, built of wood, white-washed, and with a wide shingle roof; at the east end, as if in contrast to the church, was the saloon and local place of entertainment. On this day that was to witness Dark Fury's debut as a circus horse, the place had become the focal point for those who had unexpectedly descended upon the town for the event.

As he rode slowly down the main street about mid-day, Kirk Merrett saw several Indians lounging on the veranda of the saloon, noticing with interest that a bunch of lean mustangs were tethered to the hitching post.

The animals had the appearance of having been on the trail since daybreak, for they were dusty and still spirited as if they had not yet recovered from their long trek. Quite a number of them had the stain of lather on their chests and flanks as if, amongst other things, they had been ridden hard.

Kirk lost no time in identifying the Indians who had been in the circus audience the previous evening. They were standing a little apart from the others, short, wiry fellows with sullen faces. They carried guns in their belts, and Kirk wondered if their presence in the locality meant trouble for somebody or other.

Reaching the western end of the main street, he wheeled his horse about and rode slowly back to the saloon. It was almost as though the town had become unbearably overpopulated. Folk jostled one another as they passed to and fro, mustangs were hitched in the most unlikely places, while quite a number of canvas-covered wagons were drawn up where they could be left unattended.

Kirk found it difficult to recall when he had seen such a crowd in a western township before. It was obvious that there was a heavy influx of visitors from parts well outside the trading limits of the town. Some were cowboys, possibly from Nevada, some mere horse-wranglers. It seemed that news of an exciting character had been the means of bringing them together, and Kirk felt old Tom Burke had been right after all when he said that Dark Fury would draw men from miles around to see him.

On the other hand, judging from the number of Indians present, he wondered if maybe there was not some other more significant reason behind it all. Apart from the Indians he had seen in the circus the previous night, there were some of other tribes – Umatillas from Oregon, a couple of Shoshones from Idaho, and some half-dozen or more Utes from central Utah mingling with a similar number of Piutes. There was also the usual motley gathering of half-breeds who, more likely than not, were experienced horse-thieves.

The lad decided to make a few discreet enquiries, and felt that he couldn't do better than to attempt questioning the Indians who had already made the acquaintance of the stallion.

He reined in his horse directly opposite the saloon, and dismounting, sauntered slowly over to the group of sullen-faced Cœur D'Alenes.

'How do?' he said, addressing the one he judged to be the leader of the party.

The Indian showed no surprise at being greeted by a complete stranger. He merely inclined his head in acknowledgement, but when he looked searchingly into Kirk's eyes, the lad had the distinct impression of being silently examined by a man who could almost read his innermost thoughts. Kirk could not remember having met any man who interested him more. He returned the look unflinchingly.

'What you want of me?' the Indian asked quietly.

Despite the quietness in his voice, the question was direct, demanding as direct an answer.

'I wuz kinda wonderin' if you knew anythin' about the stallion, Dark Fury?' Kirk replied without hesitation.

In the short pause that followed his words, Kirk sensed a subtle change in the Indian's face. He sensed too that his reply had been like a stone thrown into a pool, ruffling the hitherto quiet mien of the others. The moment was tense.

'Why you ask?'

There was no longer any expression in the Indian's eyes. They appeared exceptionally dark, giving no clue whatever to the thoughts they hid.

'I noticed you in the circus last night,' Kirk answered, 'an' it kinda struck me you were mighty interested when Tom Burke announced his name.'

'So?'

Disconcerted, Kirk shrugged his shoulders. He was suddenly aware of a strange sense of defeat welling up in him. That one word, uttered so nonchalantly, seemed to indicate that the Indian did not propose answering his original question. In the very moment that he thought thus, he was confounded by the man saying with emphasis in his voice: 'You bin good to wild hoss, so maybe me tell. . . .'

All Kirk could do was stare at the fellow in surprise.

'How come you to say that I've bin good to Dark Fury?' he managed to ask, his very tones still echoing the surprise he felt.

'He ain't bin here over long, an' I've only done what any man would have done who likes hosses.'

The Indian bowed slightly, then replied gravely:

'We of the Cœur D'Alenes know many things. We great people, with friends in many places. Dark Fury trapped by bad men who bring him here. They use much whip on him. You give him friendship. . . . That good for wild hoss, so Washakie, he tell what he know. . . .'

27

'Did the stallion ever belong to your tribe?' Kirk broke in, unable to check his rising curiosity.

The Indian's eyes were fixed steadily upon him; now, they held a glimmer of light as if the shadow in them had gone with his willingness to speak.

His next words, however, were in the nature of a rebuke.

'Like all white men, you impatient.' Then shaking his head, he said: 'Wild hoss belong to no tribe. . . . Him big boss of Lost Canyon where there are many mares an' much gold. No man but Indian ever find Lost Canyon.'

'The men who caught Dark Fury must have found it?' Kirk said.

'No man but Indian know way to Lost Canyon. Wild hoss caught out in sagebrush country where he has fathered many hosses. All Cœur D'Alene hosses come from big boss stallion who was named Dark Fury by great chieftain of my people.'

For the first time since the conversation, Kirk heard the note of pride in the Indian's voice. He felt too, that he was about to learn something of great importance, and looked at Washakie with an intentness he could not keep hidden.

'Me no show the way to Lost Canyon,' the fellow said slowly. 'Me only want to help big boss stallion whom our chieftain named. If hoss remain, one day he kill the bad men. . . .'

Only then did the Indian's eyes change. The glimmer of light in them became the warm flash of fire. His dark face was no longer expressionless. It was queerly alive, no longer locked in primeval apathy. It was as if, in spirit if not in body, the Indian had departed from this small Mormon township and had returned to the wild uplands of canyons and storm-shaped crags where once the stallion, Dark Fury, had dwelt with others of his kind.

Almost instinctively, Kirk found himself caught and held by the strange fascination he discovered in Washakie's eyes and face, and, as not so long since he had found himself dreaming of places he too had known and wished he had visited with the stallion, so now did he know himself to be of a kindred spirit with the Indian. . . . A dreamer, maybe . . . a searcher, perhaps, of those far horizons where the wind and man roamed free . . . the Lost Canyon country. . . .

The only trouble was, he had no idea in which direction the canyon lay.

Even so, he felt the old lawlessness come back to him, but when he made to speak further with Washakie, the fellow turned away, and with his companions, entered the saloon.

Kirk knew then that the Indian did not want to speak any more with him.

Riding back to the showground, Kirk had the feeling that he had not seen the last of Washakie or his companions. Indeed, he considered that if it were not for the interest other people were taking in them on the veranda, Washakie might have continued the conversation, despite his obvious reluctance to speak about Lost Canyon itself.

It was on the problem of the so-called lost canyon that Kirk pondered most. Quite clearly, Washakie had seen into the workings of his mind when he said so impressively 'Me no show the way to Lost Canyon', and what was more, he meant it. Nevertheless, in that one remark, so much else lay hidden. It told of the Indian's knowledge of the ways of the white man and his greed for gold. Kirk felt that Washakie would do everything possible to ensure that the fabulous canyon remained for ever undiscovered.

More important just now, however, was the Indian's intention to render some service to the stallion. Just how he proposed doing it was completely beyond Kirk's comprehension. That he would find a way, Kirk had not the slightest doubt.

The mere fact that Washakie had known all that was happening to the horse, and was appreciative of the little Kirk had been able to achieve to lessen the stallion's suffering, was a sure indication that he knew a deal more besides, and was possibly as well informed of the happenings within the sanctum of Tom Burke's caravan office.

Kirk supposed that he ought to warn Burke, but feeling that the Indian had no direct quarrel with the circus proprietor, he decided to keep quiet and watch events which, he felt, would in all probability reach some sort of climax that very evening.

Never, it seemed, had the sun travelled westward with such a crimson glow as it did that afternoon; never before had the Mormon township seemed so crowded with perspiring humanity and fretful mustangs. When the afternoon had finally given way to a very sultry evening, there was the thin tinkling of the piano in the saloon, accompanied by sudden bursts of laughter and discordant attempts at singing.

All the while the red glow of the sunset spilled down upon the main street and upon the shacks and stores. Way over, a few wisps of dust trailed across the desert and were caught by a contrary breeze. The mountains of the far eastern horizon were temporarily gilded by the last of the evening light, and even as the shadows gathered in the hollows between them, so did the peaks catch a little of the crimson glow that by now had entirely invaded the township.

A brace of sage grouse came flying low over the desert, and with a croak, made for the corral where Dark Fury, having just eaten his evening meal of oats, stood listening to the sounds that heralded the awakening of Burke's Circus.

The sage grouse alighted in the sour grass less than a dozen yards away. Dark Fury, however, did not heed them. His attitude was one of nervous anticipation.

The showground was besieged early that night by the most cosmopolitan crowd that had ever sought the doubtful delights of a third-rate circus and the attendant side-shows that went with it. White folk rubbed shoulders with redskin, and half-breed with Mexican. People thronged up and down, and the showmen, to attract them, proclaimed that theirs was the greatest show on earth. Hucksters too did an excellent trade, selling herbs made from prairie grass, and wine made from some obscure weed that was as pungent as it was strong. Indeed, all the fun of a middle-west show was to be had that night at Burke's Circus showground. Cowboys, fresh off the ranges, tried their luck at the various games of skill set up to take the money of the unwary and inexperienced. Others, encouraged by their companions, swaggered into the boxing booths only to return a little later saddened and sore, but some, a trifle wiser.

Most of the caged animals were visited by the more curious type of individual, even Bruno, Tom Burke's favourite bear, was given more than his usual share of attention.

Remarkable though it was, Dark Fury who was to be the star performer that night, was left very much alone, although many were the glances that were cast in his direction. Not even the most rowdy of the cowboys sought out the stallion standing watchful and highly strung in the corral.

It seemed that word had somehow got around that the horse was best left alone. Whether it was Luke Unwin and his friends who had spread the idea, or Washakie and his companions, was not quite clear, even to Kirk who was carefully watching the proceedings.

One thing, however, was quite certain. More than one cowboy was heard to declare that a stallion the like of Dark Fury was far better on an open range rounding up mares than parading a circus ring.

Kirk, listening and watching, could sense that there was a tense atmosphere whenever Dark Fury's name was mentioned, and he could not help feeling that despite old Tom Burke's optimism, the stallion's circus debut was not going to be the success the showman had visualised.

Then a little before the evening performance was due to begin, the huge tent was ablaze with lamplight. The hucksters and outside showmen ceased their shouting, and a great crowd began to gather for admission to the Big Top. A most significant factor, Kirk thought, was that there were no women visible amongst the crowd. Suddenly, for the first time that evening, Washakie and his Indian friends made their appearance in the showground. Till then, they and other members of the redskin clan had remained in the vicinity of the saloon.

Under the spread of the Big Top it was stuffy, which emphasised the animal smells peculiar to it. The lampglow did but serve to uncover the abject nakedness and poverty of what Tom Burke fondly imagined was a magnificent arena. Even the big ring itself was little better than a sandy patch enclosed by a rope held in place by stakes with bits of coloured material on them for bunting.

The seats were rough wooden forms which, in a matter of minutes from the admittance of the audience, creaked and groaned as if about to collapse. It was a most unusual audience too that night. From a rowdy gathering of folk out to enjoy the unexpected thrills of a showground, the moment the circus tent was entered all sense of gaiety was lost. The entire audience, comprising only men, sat quiet and upright on the forms, uttering scarcely a word one to the other, and seeming curiously tense. Only now and again was heard the restless shifting of feet.

Four sets of forms adjacent to the big ring were unoccupied. Despite the crush to gain entrance to the Big Top, nobody seemed anxious to take possession of them.

Then, a few minutes before Burke came to announce the programme for the night, Washakie and his friends entered, moving silently down one of the narrow gangways, and seating themselves on the vacant forms. The Indians' solemn faces were specially noticed by all who watched their slow passage to their seats.

It was then that a whisper, started at the back of the arena, passed, like a ripple of flame, from seat to seat.

'They sure mean business!'

No more was whispered than that, no further word added because nobody knew for certain what the Cœur D'Alenes intended doing in this matter of a stallion who, as far as was known, was anybody's hoss ... leastways, if you had the wit to catch him which apparently somebody had.

There was a strong rumour, none the less, that since Dark Fury had, at some time or another, received special consideration from a Cœur D'Alene chieftain, certain members of the tribe had been commanded to see that the hoss was returned to the range where he belonged. That, as most folk saw it was the only reason to account for so many Cœur D'Alenes being so far from the tribal reservation.

More than the stallion, perhaps, it was the range he came from that really mattered. There was scarcely one amongst the audience that night who would not have given all he possessed just to know the exact location of the range. All had heard tales concerning the lost canyon that was believed to lie somewhere in wild hoss country up north, and like all such tales, embellishments to the truth were made each time the story was repeated.

All further conjectures as to the Indians' intentions and the where-abouts of Lost Canyon were immediately forgotten the moment Tom Burke took his place in the ring and glanced uneasily around.

Contrary to all circus traditions, his appearance was greeted by a deep silence. He could not understand it, and was plagued by the disquieting thought that before the night was over, he was going to experience trouble.

He squared his shoulders and stared at his audience. His look defied anybody to interrupt him.

He then read out his announcements as quickly as possible, and bowing, signified to the four pieces of brass to sound an appropriate chord. It seemed to him as he left the ring that the chord was a little off key and that the big drum, to give the final flourish, rolled a little too loudly.

He shook his head and wondered.

Gripping the lapels of his elaborate jacket, Burke decided to stand close to Kirk in one of the gangways and await the first animal act to make its entry.

It was Bruno, his bear who, on reaching the ring, roared and grimaced to a totally unresponsive audience.

Thus commenced the most memorable of Tom Burke's entertainments, with the stallion, Dark Fury, as its most outstanding event.

Chapter Four

Burke thought Bruno was doing very well indeed. The bear responded, without hesitation, to everything his trainer said. Even so, the animal seemed completely unable to set off the first spark necessary to fire the imaginations of those who watched him. There was not a single laugh at what Burke considered was Bruno's funniest antics. Nor was there any sign of interest and approbation when the bear successfully aped his trainer.

The showman thought desperately: 'What's the matter with thim, the varmints. . . . Maybe when Bruno starts dancin', it'll be different. Sure, the boyos 'll laugh then, sure enough. . . .'

At last, and not an instant too soon Burke felt, the awaited moment came, with the huge bear, dressed as a clown gambolling clumsily around the ring, followed by the trainer who was whooping and doing his best to rouse the audience to some response.

The effort was to no avail.

After a further three minutes of strained silence, Bruno's performance came to an end, and the bear, grimacing and bowing, left the ring to the accompaniment of the band, playing as discordantly as ever.

As the trainer bustled past Burke, he murmured: 'It's a quare crowd we have in tonight, boss, an' no mistake. . . . Very quare. . . .'

Burke made no reply.

The next act was the mountain lions which usually roused everybody to a pitch of wild excitement, due, in the main, Burke supposed,

34

to the uncertainty of their tempers when faced with a crowd. On this particular evening, their entry into the arena along the canvas-sided gangway passed without mishap. For once, the wheels of the huge cage containing them revolved easily over the uneven ground, and the animals did not suffer their usual indignity of being hurtled from one side to the other as their conveyance creaked its way into the ring.

When the cage was suitably placed so that every member of the audience from the slant of the canvas roof to the sand-strewn floor surrounding the ring could witness all that went on, the lions' trainer and owner stepped into the arena. He was a big, loose-limbed Dane, clad only in singlet and shorts and armed with nothing more lethal than a strong hide whip.

After a flourish of the whip, and an elaborate bow, he prepared to put the beasts through their paces. As was their habit, the lions expressed their disapproval in loud roars that went echoing into the sultry night air.

In the corral, Dark Fury bristled with mingled anger and fear at sound of their voices. Not even the hardships of the last few months had been able to erase from his animal consciousness the bitter memories so closely allied to the creatures who had once been his greatest enemies. Despite the limitations imposed on him by his captivity, Dark Fury's close kinship with the wild had not been seriously weakened, but in many ways had been more strongly emphasised by reason of his renewed association with animals who had represented danger in that free life which man had taken from him.

The stallion suddenly snorted and stamped his feet as he recognised the figures of Luke Unwin and two of his henchmen approaching.

Unwin was in no fit mood to handle the horse that night. Irritated by the knowledge that Enos Wills had made himself scarce for reasons best known to himself, this irritation was communicated to Dark Fury the very instant he approached with bridle and rope.

Maitland appeared as a gesticulating shadow behind Luke.

As Unwin reached up impatiently, Maitland whispered urgently: 'Steady, boss . . . steady!'

35

Unwin grunted.

'Steady, you say?'

He made a quick lunge forward, and in a trice, had the bridle over Dark Fury's head, and the bit securely between his teeth.

'That's how you do it,' he grunted. Then sharply, 'Look out!'

The stallion reared, and from out of the gloom came the sharp crack of a whip as Corson, emulating the absent Wills, tried to subdue any move the horse might make to become over-spirited. With the quick action of Corson behind him, Dark Fury plunged violently. Then as Unwin managed to bring his head down sharply, he ceased to fret at the bit and became still.

'Do you think he'll do?' Corson whispered.

Unwin laughed.

'Sure, he'll do,' he answered. 'He ain't got to show off with tricks an' sichlike, same as Bruno. All we got to do is see he keeps steady.'

'You shud have given him 'is trainin' in the big tent,' Maitland remarked.

'Sure, he's right there Luke,' Corson joined in. 'That's jest what ole man Burke said.'

Unwin laughed again.

'Sure, that's what ole man Burke said,' he replied. 'The ole feller's always sayin' sumthin' or other, but he don't know everythin'. I've kept the hoss out of the tent fer one good reason. He'll be one hell of a curious crittur when he gits inside there, with the crowd an' all. That's what we want ... fer him to look the best hoss ever; an' he'll be that all right, with his head up an' his eyes glarin'. ... Yippee. ... He'll be the greatest hoss seen in these parts anyway. ... Enos 'll miss sumthin' not seein' him tonight. ...'

The enthusiasm in his voice impressed his companions.

'Mebbe you've gotten sumthin', after all,' Maitland agreed reluctantly.

'I sure have. You'll see!'

Luke gripped the bridle tightly.

'Watch them Indians,' Corson broke in, suddenly. 'You know what folk 'eve bin sayin' in the saloon.'

The knuckles on Unwin's hand gleamed white in the darkness.

'The Indians won't do anythin. . . . The hoss is ours. . . . We caught him. . . .'

'All right, boss! Jest keep your eyes open. That's all. . . .'

'Sure! Sure! I'll do jest that. Mebbe you'd better do the same.'

Unwin slid his fingers along the rope attached to the bridle until they were within an inch or so of the bit. By so doing, he managed to have complete control of the stallion's head and was thus able to check immediately any sudden move the horse might make.

'He'll do fine,' Luke breathed. 'He'll sure send them all crazy when they see him. He's a great hoss all right. . . .'

Then using his free hand in such a manner that Dark Fury could not see what he was doing, he snatched the whip from Corson's grasp.

'Release the tether,' he ordered.

'Be careful, boss,' Corson warned.

'Release it!' was the swift reply.

With Maitland close at his heels, Corson did as Luke commanded.

A quiver of excitement rippled along Dark Fury's back as he felt the sudden falling away of the check rope which, since he had been enclosed in the corral, had limited his ranging propensities. Nevertheless, he had the sense not to make any immediate move. He was full of distrust for Unwin, and was sharply conscious of the hurt of the bit in his mouth. It was the rasping of the bit that told him that while Unwin held his head down, he had to obey every gesture the man made, every action being determined by the tug of the bridle which, in turn, loosened or tightened the pieces of steel between his teeth.

Luke Unwin then proceeded to lead him towards the Big Top, closely followed by the others.

The lion act ended in the same strained silence that had marked its beginning, and the cage was being wheeled out of the circus arena when Unwin approached the canvas alleyway with Dark Fury.

There was a hiss of irritation from the Dane who was perspiring freely.

'Over-anxious, ain't you?'

Luke grunted, but was compelled to ignore what he felt was meant to be an offensive remark, for the rank scent of the lions was stinging the stallion's nostrils; he noted the sudden attempt Dark Fury made to spring a little to one side and gain his head.

In a sudden anxiety, he gripped the bridle more tenaciously than ever, causing the horse to grate his teeth on the bit.

The cage was hauled at last into the outer gloom of the showground, but the stench remained, and when Luke led Dark Fury under the tent flap and waited in the gangway while Burke made the necessary announcement, he could feel the stallion trembling against him.

Then Burke's voice came at him like a booming note echoing from under the spread of the Big Top, and he was momentarily aware that he had been joined by Maitland and Corson, the latter whispering: 'What's 'e sayin'?'

Before either Luke or Maitland could reply, Burke's closing words were clearly heard. . . . 'Presentin' the great wild stallion . . . Dark Fury!'

The same heavy silence that had greeted the previous announcement was perhaps a little more heavily accentuated by the dramatic intensity of the showman's tones when uttering the stallion's name.

For the first time since he had embarked on such a hazardous career, Luke Unwin experienced a surge of fear that brought a clammy moisture to his hands and a chill to his usually overheated body. It was unnatural, he thought, for a crowd to be so quiet. Mebbe, after all, there was goin' to be trouble like Bill an' Tim said. Mebbe, Enos knew sumthin' when he said he was quittin' for the night.

His thoughts ranged backwards and forwards as he stood waiting for his call, then he was aware of having no thoughts at all as Burke suddenly loomed up, saying angrily: 'Come on. . . . Quit the dreamin'. They're waitin', an' arrah! me boyo! Ye'd better be good. It's a quare mob we have in tonight. . . . A mighty quare mob if ye ask me my opinion. . . .'

Then as Luke still hesitated, he waved his arms, shouting: 'Go on. . . . Git movin'. . . .'

Luke moved forward mechanically, holding Dark Fury's head well down. He was conscious that his heart was playing tricks on him, and that his legs weren't so steady as they might be. He thought chaotically 'Hell, but I'm sorry I started this business. . . .' He looked back over his shoulder for Bill and Tim as if seeking their support, and cursed silently that Enos wasn't with them.

Burke, however, had checked the others' attempt to enter the ring, and in another second, Luke found himself walking into the yellow lamplight of the arena, with the harsh blare of the band sounding in his ears. He couldn't see a thing for a moment, and was only conscious of a restless movement from Dark Fury. It was not until the movement was repeated that he realised the horse was making a determined effort to get his head free.

Luke, pulling himself together, tried to bring the stallion completely under control. Along with the scent of the mountain lions was now mingled the smell of close-packed humanity, and an even stronger tang of freshly laid sawdust.

So many varying scents only unnerved the stallion to a greater degree, and digging his hooves into the sawdust, he refused to obey Unwin's sharply uttered words of command.

Meanwhile, Tom Burke with young Merrett at his side, stood in the gangway, watching helplessly. Both seemed conscious of an impending disaster.

Luke began to lose his temper. Tugging at the bridle, he shouted angrily: 'Come on you quitter!' and then with cruel intent, raised the whip. As he did so, a voice rang out.

'You better stop, mister!'

The next instant, Luke found himself surrounded by Indians who had leapt quietly into the ring. There was a muffled roar of approval from the crowd – the first that night – and Burke and Merrett glanced instinctively around for some sign of the sheriff. Even as they made a move to hurry off for assistance, somebody said 'You no leave big tepee,' and they discovered to their surprise that they too were hemmed in by Indians.

Burke's face seemed to shrink; in fact, his whole figure seemed to have shrivelled so much in the last few minutes that his clothes no longer fitted him.

Kirk, moved by pity, told him not to worry.

The showman rolled his eyes in despair.

In the meantime, Dark Fury had succeeded in wrenching his head free. Luke, defying the Indians, endeavoured to regain his hold on the bridle; but too late. The Indian, Washakie, with a movement so quick that Luke scarcely saw it, got hold of the rope, and with nimble fingers, began slipping the bridle off the stallion's head.

Whilst Dark Fury was trembling in every limb, he yet suffered the Indian to touch him. All at once he knew that his mouth was free of the iron that had caused him such discomfort. His head went up immediately, and he ceased to tremble. Moreover, he showed not the slightest sign of fear when Washakie attempted to place a lead rope over his neck.

By now, the entire audience was on its feet, making no effort to join the Indians, but watching intently everything they did.

Unwin was held by two of Washakie's companions, while others of the Cœur D'Alene tribe made a pathway to the main entrance, and Dark Fury was led quietly out of the ring.

The Indians were everywhere. They stood at what were clearly strategic points, and even as Luke Unwin, struggling violently, shouted 'Stop him. ... He's stealin' my hoss. ...' so did Washakie, without any hindrance whatever, lead Dark Fury out of the Big Top into the silence of the night.

Not more than a minute passed before the Big Top was in an uproar. The spectators, formerly sullen and unresponsive, now started to shout and jeer. Some even attempted to sever the guy ropes holding the big tent into position while others began to throw the forms about.

Burke and his friends tried to quell what had become a riot, and as they ran to and fro gesticulating and shouting for order, the Indians vanished as silently as they had appeared. By the time the Big Top swayed and collapsed with a hundred people or more struggling and screaming beneath the canvas, they had mounted their mustangs and were gone.

On the edge of the desert, Washakie, still holding Dark Fury by the lead rope, paused and listened to the rising tumult, made more hideous by the roars of the now terrified animals.

One of the tribe came riding up, leading his mustang.

'Quick! The sheriff . . . he come with posse. . . .'

Washakie's dark eyes flashed with relief at the sight of his own horse.

As he swung himself up into the saddle, the rope holding Dark Fury fell a trifle slack. Suddenly, the stallion wriggled his head free. With a backward spring, he reared, and then plunged forward. He was off . . . off across the arid desert, dark beneath the stars . . . heading north-west to where the mountains marked the borders of the Great Salt Lake of Utah.

At the very moment of his escape, a great blaze illuminated the sky.

Burke's Circus was going up in flames!

Chapter Five

The angry glare of the fire spread fanwise across the desert as Dark
Fury made his spectacular bid for freedom. In the flickering glow,
the undulating stretches of arid sand reddened and darkened alterna-
tively. Each hollow became, for a moment, an immense amphitheatre, each ridge, a league-long finger searching out towards the
horizon. No fire, however great, could completely bridge the enormous distance that lay betwixt the Mormon township and the eastern
limits of the so-called 'bad lands'. Only the fierce glare of sunset
could touch those distant mountains that fell back, range upon
range, to form the western wall of the vast basin in which lay the
remains of the salt lake that had once completely covered the deserts
of Utah.

Dark Fury went racing away with his tail streaming out behind
him and his mane tossing like black wings beating wildly. Although
there was no discernible track across the desert, his feet seemed to fly
with an inborn certainty over a trail that had possibly existed many
hundreds of years before, when the white man was but a dream, and
the Utes – the native Indian tribe of Utah – plied their wares and
rode their mustangs from the regions of the salt lake to the more
fertile lands of Nevada.

The sand was still warm beneath the surface, and the only noticeable change in the temperature would be apparent a little after
midnight when it usually grew cold until the spin of the earth
brought another day smouldering on the skyline.

As he forged on, maintaining a quick, easy pace, Dark Fury passed miles of low greasewood and patches of yellow sage which marked the way to the first perceptible rise in the desert floor. Not once did he deviate from that hidden trail he followed which went straight as a drawn line across the miles of barren country to the far distant mountains.

Well behind him now, continued to blaze the fire that was bringing total ruin to Burke's Circus. The reflection, while still spreading out fanwise over the barren land, was not quite so fierce as when Dark Fury went careering off into the gloom, for the Big Top was no more, and only the rude interior furnishings, the wooden forms and similar items, continued to blaze with vigour.

The stallion, spurred on by the repeated flickers of light that seemed to reach out, touch him, then pass on, did not slacken in his running. He soon got over the first strain on his muscles by the unaccustomed pace he set, and when he finally got his second wind, his movement was once again the rhythm of limbs and sinews working in complete unison.

After an hour's steady running, he permitted himself to drop into an even trot, having struck a network of washes that had once, in the rainy season, held water, but were now as dry as bleached bones.

The main wash – a deep ridge running due east – was the one he followed, for once again, his hooves seemed to respond to the call of the ancient trail that lay hidden beneath the countless siftings of sand. Gone now were the patches of sage and the sparse scatterings of greasewood. It was pure alkaline desert he traversed now, without any surface growth whatever and certainly with no trace of fresh water. The few red gashes that appeared occasionally beside the trail were as dry as the network of washes that had indicated the beginning of the barren lands.

The slow rise in the floor of the desert continued, and the atmosphere was gradually cooling. Soon there was a trickle of wind that brought particles of dust spinning from off the surrounding ridges. High in the purple vault of the sky, the bright stars rolled away from the east where a faint ripple of light brought warning to the stallion that a new day was not far off.

At last Dark Fury halted, and breathing heavily, stood listening intently.

Nothing could he hear save the repeated whisper of the almost contrary wind, and the faint movement of sand when caught in its sudden grasp and flung from one ridge to another: and as he turned and faced resolutely the direction from which he had come, all Dark Fury could see was the shadowed depression he had followed, slipping away into a gloom that finally engulfed it. Of the fire that had marked the end of Burke's Circus, not even a flicker remained.

It was almost as though the darkest of dark nights had gathered where the Big Top had once stood waving its tattered pennants to the stars. . . .

For quite five minutes – short indeed in the eternity of time the desert had known – Dark Fury stood gazing back along the wavering gully of the wash, his ears pricked forward a little, and his nostrils flaring the atmosphere. Boldly alert, he yet stood with hereditary grace, his fine lines and dark mane and tail etched against the tawny uprising of the sand ridge. No gloom, temporarily amassed in a hollow, could altogether obliterate the shape of one who was surely the very personification of darkness.

All the while, the frail bursts of wind which, on the higher ridges, possessed sufficient strength to scatter the sand before it, but which, in the protection of the wash, was scarcely the breath of a sigh, touched the stallion with fingers so light that he hardly felt their impress upon him.

Yet, he was not entirely unresponsive to the probing of the wind. Something inside him exulted, for the wind had ever been his ally save, perhaps, on the one occasion when he had been betrayed into the hands of those who made him captive. Even on that one occasion the fault had been his own, for he had been standing headlong to the wind, and it could give no warning of that which it had not passed.

The lesson he learnt on that grim night was one he was not likely to forget. Not for an instant did his nose stop testing the air, and although his body was motionless, his head was constantly turning from left to right, each pulse of wind being thoroughly investigated.

Whilst he was reassured time and time again that no taint of man was being carried to him, he was nervously inclined, for neither did the wind bring to him the scent he wanted most to pick up – the tang of water.

There came to him then the sharp knowledge, bordering on to fear, that he would have to journey a great distance before he was likely to find a clear running river. In another hour, the sun would be up.

Dark Fury tossed his head and whinnied. He swung around and clambered out of the defile to stand on the ridge along which the wind seemed to be shaping its course.

The dawn, by now, was gathering in a riot of colour all along the eastern horizon. The sky with its countless stars paled swiftly into a greyness that lasted but a few seconds before becoming part of that vibrant colour.

Once again the stallion tossed his head, then, hugging the ridge, was off again, trotting at an easy pace, running full into the cool breeze that refreshed him as he went.

Above the desert, the stars went out one by one, like distant candles extinguished by a hidden hand; a wisp of cloud burned blood red over what had been a water-hole but was now a dried-up hollow. Then the sun came up, fierce and golden like a brazen shield to dazzle the eyes of all, but an eagle, who dared to look at it: and the trickle of wind whimpered and died.

Panting, Dark Fury continued on his way. With the breaking of that fiery dawn, he had glimpsed, a long way off, those mountains that he must reach; and they showed dark against the gold, but with no ridges or valleys discernible. Only the peaks stood out in that transfiguration of the dawn ... very low down on that far horizon, but nevertheless, quite distinctly visible. It was like a glimpse of a land of promise ... a serrated skyline that held in the hidden canyons the life-giving water that had been denied to the alkaline desert that was now a glaring waste in the harsh sunlight.

For the best part of two hours, Dark Fury kept up the even trotting until he was forced to leave the ridge and take once again to the depression of the wash, where it seemed a little less hot and where his feet responded more easily to the call of that hidden trail he sensed lay beneath it.

By the afternoon, his trotting was no more than a quickly paced walk. He was weary and the heat was rapidly sapping his main reserves of strength.

The slow hours wore away towards the approach of another night. It seemed that the sun was long a-westering that evening, but at last it disappeared behind the canyons of Nevada, and the crimson afterglow, reaching out in long rivers of translucent light, touched those eastern crags of Utah that Dark Fury longed to reach.

In every way, the stallion was nigh to a point of exhaustion. He had driven himself too hard in a vain attempt to reach those eastern hills. Moreover, his throat had become parched, and his need for water was greater than his desire for rest.

Thus, he still continued to press on, his head drooping and his legs hesitant as his hooves sank into the sand.

The sunset died out in the west, and the afterglow departed from those mountains guarding the great salt lake of Utah. Before they had completely vanished into the night that was fast dropping down upon them, they stood out for a brief moment, sharply defined and seeming much nearer than they actually were.

It was as he raised his head and came to a stumbling halt that Dark Fury saw them thus, and an eager, excited look came into his eyes. Then, even as he looked, they vanished, taken by the shadows that were rapidly advancing across the entire desert.

An hour later, the travel-weary horse came to a thin sprinkling of sage beyond which were a few stunted cacti and sun-bleached mesquite,[1] all surrounding a dried-up water-hole.

Struggling out of the depression along which he had travelled for most of the long hours of daylight, Dark Fury sought a temporary refuge amongst the groups of mesquite, and was soon sleeping from complete exhaustion.

It was a curiously quiet night, with no sound of life anywhere on the desert, although a mild breeze moved amongst the cactus and

1. Mesquite – a leguminous tree or shrub of America, with nutritious pods.

became stronger as the first light of day spilled once more over the eastern skyline.

Suddenly the desert resounded to a stallion's scream of alarm, as Dark Fury sprang to his feet, roused by the swift passage of a snake over his flanks. The horse had been hovering between a state of sleeping and waking when he experienced the first movement of the reptile beneath his brisket where the creature had been curled for warmth. Even then he did not respond immediately to the probe of fear that was flashed to his brain. The sliding of the snake across his flanks was another matter. Dark Fury was wide awake and on his feet, springing clear as the sinuous shape fell from him.

Had he not suffered the slow degradation of the long weeks in captivity, and had become highly strung as a result of his contact with man, he would have reacted altogether differently. He would not have ceased pounding the snake beneath his hooves until the creature was dead. As it was, Dark Fury turned, and before the reptile could coil and strike, the stallion was in flight, his eyes bright with the terror that lent speed to his feet and made him forgetful of the discomfort of a throat that was dry and painful.

For over an hour, he galloped without any regard for the direction he was travelling; and all the while the greyness of a new day gathered and spread into the dazzling brightness of a morning as pitiless as the other mornings that had preceded it.

The sun was once more a harsh glare in the sky when Dark Fury became aware that he was approaching a series of ridges beyond which were the stumps of long-dead cedars. There was also a thin growth of sage forming into a purple carpet as it stretched away to another more distant crest. As he pressed on, Dark Fury discovered that the various ridges were like steps, the topmost one being distinguished by a single cedar that was not dead like the stumps he had passed, but was a lone shrub that had every appearance of having struggled tenaciously for root-hold in an unrewarding soil.

Dark Fury came to a sharp halt, his nostrils flaring widely. He was finding it less difficult to breathe, and as he tested the atmosphere, he caught at last the penetrating fragrance that could only come from an abundance of cedar and sage.

His drooping spirits revived at once. He continued his struggle up the series of ridges. The ascent was gradual, but the rise in the desert elevation was more than apparent as he passed crest after crest. At last, he clambered up on to that plateau distinguished by the single cedar, and stood as if in surprise.

Before him was a small but certainly odorous forest of cedar, rising up from out of a carpet of sage. It was not upon the cedar and sage that he gazed, however, as he stood beside the dwarfed shrub that was but a sentinel of the small forest. His look was held by an enormous monumental wall of rock that rose, terrace upon terrace, less than a mile off. It did not quite possess the dignity of an impressive mountain, rising as it did to no more than two thousand feet, but it possessed some lofty pinnacles, and there seemed to be a narrow canyon thrusting in between huge walls of red rock. Moreover, its very appearance breaking so abruptly the monotony of the desert, gave it a grandeur that more than made up for its lack of height and shattered façade.

A little to the left of the canyon was a dark shaft, striking far into the bowels of the rock. To the stallion, in urgent need of respite from the glare of the desert and the heat, the spot was inviting, and he started off through the cedar and sage.

The well-defined trail led straight to the canyon; it was the beginning of that age-old trail he had instinctively traversed in the depression of the wash and which, out there in the desert, was lost for ever beneath the accumulation of sand.

Soon, that monumental wall of rock was less than a quarter of a mile away, and the sage was giving way to loose shale thinly covered by sand.

As nearer he approached, the higher did the escarpment appear to be. The lofty crags had assumed the height and splendour of cathedral spires, and high up on the shattered terraces were more shaft-like openings. Although the stallion knew it not, those openings in the rock face were once the primitive dwellings of the Indians who, in a past age, had dared the perils of the desert to carry their wares to the distant trading posts of Nevada, and who, from their homes high up on the cliffs, had worshipped the great Fire-Maker – the Sun!

It took Dark Fury some ten minutes or more to reach the mouth of the canyon where he halted, gazing along a winding trail that thrust up steeply between the leaning walls of rock. From where he stood, at the entrance to the ruinous ascent, his nostrils told him that the entire canyon was dry and barren. There was not the slightest scent of water anywhere.

At last, the stallion turned away from the canyon and made for the dark shaft-like opening he had glimpsed when back on the trail.

He advanced into the darkness cautiously, his feet moving over rubble and sand and his nostrils for ever testing the atmosphere.

Finally, while still within the reach of the light filtering from the opening of the shaft, his forefeet sank into a spongy mass, and as he paused uncertainly, he felt the slow dripping of water from the roof of the cavern.

Although there was no sound of a running stream, water dropped ceaselessly from a source somewhere in the very heart of the rock formation itself.

In a matter of seconds, Dark Fury was passing his tongue over the moistened sides of the cavern, and after an hour, the dryness of his throat was less apparent, and he felt a new vitality springing up inside him. Then towards sundown, he managed to find a patch of moss which he ate slowly, disliking its bitter flavour, but none the less chewing it to relieve the hunger he experienced.

That night, a blazing afterglow lingered long in the west, with trailing streamers of light reaching out across the desert to find a last reflection on the terraced wall of rock that had once been the home of cave-dwellers who had worshipped the sun.

Long indeed, that night, did the pinnacles of rock remain red against the clear sky, but by the time they had become dark spears reaching up to the stars, Dark Fury, the wanderer, lay sleeping close to the entrance of the shaft, enjoying for the first time in days a rest that was free from the torment of thirst and heat.

He was not entirely alone, however. An ancient vulture, the evil spirit of Sun Rock, sat unsleeping on his favourite ledge. He had witnessed the coming of many like Dark Fury, and had seen them die. . . .

Meanwhile, the stallion slept on, with no fear of death disturbing his slumbers, and with no recurring memory of those who had once held him captive.

Chapter Six

The night of Dark Fury's escape was a night likely to remain long in the memories of the folk who dwelt in the Mormon township. With the summoning of the sheriff came the swift departure of the Indians who had all but laid siege to Burke's circus.

While the sound of their mustangs' hooves was still echoing down the main street, a great roar came from the direction of the show-ground. The next thing folk knew was that a yellow glare was illuminating the entire township, throwing into relief the shacks and stores as the Big Top collapsed and went up in flames.

Almost at once the clamour of human voices became one discordant scream, and against the fantastic backcloth of fire and smoke, figures ran to and fro like puppets jerked into spasmodic movement by an invisible hand.

Somebody shouted that the circus animals had broken loose. The cry was taken up on all sides, and the now panic-stricken mob came milling from the scene of the disaster, some of the men taking refuge in the first place that presented a likely fortress against an animal invasion, others – as many as could gain admittance – crowding into the saloon where they stood behind bolted doors, some with guns held in readiness to shoot down the first creature that attempted an entry.

Although the lions were roaring with fear, only one beast came lumbering away from the showground, his huge arms raised above his head as he tried to run, closely pursued by old Tom Burke himself.

It was Bruno, the bear, frenzied at sight of the leaping flames, and, for once, completely oblivious to the shouting voice of his master.

Kirk Merrett, who had also witnessed Bruno's escape, joined in the chase. His youth was an advantage over the elder man. He quickly outstripped him, and putting in a final burst of speed, managed to get well in advance of the bear.

He could hear Bruno uttering weird cries of fear, almost like the desperate wailing of a child, so high-pitched was the animal's voice. He thought vaguely that no matter the cost, he must save the bear from further hurt and alarm and he made a quick, decisive turn. His action took the bear completely by surprise, and at the very moment when the animal was about to make a manoeuvre calculated to take him in the direction of the saloon veranda.

Kirk leaped forward, then upward, the palms of his hands pressing against Bruno's chest.

The bear was momentarily thrown off his balance, and stumbled. As he did so, the young man, with surprising agility, made another upward thrust and succeeded in getting a grip on the chain that dangled from the bear's collar.

Gritting his teeth, he hung on wildly. He could feel the animal tensing himself to take the additional strain; he became aware of being lifted off his feet, his body swinging ominously towards Bruno's outstretched arms.

Then Tom Burke reached him.

'Bruno! Bruno!' the Irishman shouted breathlessly.

The bear jerked himself upright, his head half-turned as he recognised at last the authority in his master's voice.

Burke made the most of the opportunity he had gained. He also reached up for the chain, and getting a firm grip on it, motioned Kirk to release his hold.

The very instant Bruno found himself under the control of his master, he lost much of the fear that had sent him careering from the showground. He ceased to be the crazed beast that had cried like a child, and stood waiting for Burke to lead him to a place of safety.

'That was a near thing,' Kirk gasped, grinning up at Burke.

'It sure was,' the showman answered. Then turning his whole

attention to the bear, and speaking to him softly, he led the creature to a quiet spot behind the caravans where he was unlikely to be molested. After tethering him securely, and tossing him a truss of hay, he hurried off with Kirk to witness the final ruin of the circus.

By now, most of the circus hands had managed to haul the animal cages to a point some distance away from the fire; they then proceeded to move the vans in which most of them lived.

There was little grumbling, and everybody worked with a will. For more than a couple of hours, the men laboured to save what properties remained, but it was well after midnight before the conflagration showed signs of burning itself out, and even then, occasional bursts of flame gave a grotesque appearance to the blackened mass that had once been a place of entertainment.

Both Kirk and Tom Burke worked as hard as the next man, never sparing themselves until the last movable item had been put out of reach of smoke and cinder. All this time, the showman said scarcely a word, having already decided in his mind to make a fresh start in the morning.

He smiled ruefully as he bent forward, giving his entire attention to the lifting of a large coil of rope. As he straightened up, with the rope held in his arms, he thought: 'The ole tent had seen better days, that it had ...' and recalled that for over a year he had intended replacing it. He chuckled softly as he carried the rope to the pile of miscellaneous material close to the caravans. Faith! it 'ud be a grand tent he'd have next time. A bigger tent, with flags an' buntin' to give it colour. It might cost him a pretty packet, but it would pay off in the long run. He still had all his animals with the possible exception of Dark Fury who, as he saw it now, had been the black talisman of fate, bringing disaster not only to the circus, but to those who had handled him.

He then realised that Luke Unwin and his companions were nowhere visible, and mentioned the fact to Kirk.

Kirk had not seen them either, but hazarded a guess as to where they could be found. He nodded in the direction of the saloon.

Burke grunted and accepted the men's absence with a shrug of his shoulders.

'I alwis thought they were four no-goods, anyway,' he remarked.

'All of 'em hoss thieves if you ask me,' Kirk replied.

The showman looked at him reflectively.

'Mebbe you're right at that,' he said slowly. 'One of 'em wuz missin' tonight too when he shud 'ave bin close at hand.' Then in a different tone of voice, he added: 'You kinda liked that hoss, didn't you?'

'I sure did,' Kirk answered.

'I expect them Indians 'ave got him now.'

'Mebbe. They'll sure treat him better, anyway.'

'Sure. Sure. They'll do that all right. Them other critturs treated him some tough, that they did. . . .'

As he resumed his lifting and carrying, he wondered why he had agreed to give the stallion a place in the circus programme. Mebbe, it was Unwin's plausible line of talk that had persuaded him.

'The last of the great wild stallions,' the feller had said.

The old showman blew noisily through his lips.

Sure . . . a fine hoss . . . the very best. . . . Not even in his native Ireland could he remember having seen a better; an' faith! there was some good hoss flesh way back in the Emerald Isle. . . . Pity he hadn't persuaded Unwin to sell Dark Fury. Then mebbe he'd still have had the Big Top . . . an' th' hoss too. . . .

His thoughts ran on and on until he realised that the night was for the most part spent, and that the new day was not far off.

He suddenly called a halt to further efforts of salvage.

'Best quit now, boys,' he shouted.

The men, exceedingly weary, required no second bidding, and were soon departing in twos and threes to their various vans. At last only Tom Burke and Kirk remained, standing within a few feet of the smouldering rubbish that had once been a tent.

Neither spoke. They just stared down at the glowing embers, the elder man thinking once again of the fine Big Top he would raise at the first opportunity, the younger man thinking only of the stallion who had vanished completely . . . gone, nobody knew quite where . . . but certainly taken by the Indians who would see to it that he never again returned to the ignominy of circus life.

Kirk suddenly felt the desire to be alone. A hundred and one problems were fretting at his mind.

'I think I'll be turnin' in, boss,' he said abruptly.

There was that in Kirk's voice that roused the protective instinct in the elder man. He gave a half-shy response to it by placing his hand on the young fellow's shoulder, remarking kindly: 'You've done well by me this night, so you have. Sure, be away with yez, an' sleep well. . . .'

With an ill-concealed smile, the showman turned and made off to his own van, leaving Kirk still standing beside the glowing embers that were being fanned into a new life by the penetrating breeze coming in from off the desert.

Shivering a little as if at some chill come suddenly into his blood, Kirk prepared to follow. Suddenly his body tautened and his heart quickened its beat. A faint sound held him motionless; then a shadow moved in his direction.

To his surprise, he recognised Washakie.

'Say, ain't you takin' a chance showin' up here?' he questioned in a sharp whisper.

The Indian stood but a couple of paces away, his eyes shining as they reflected the glow of the smouldering ash. To Kirk, he was no more than the dark shadow of a man, recognisable only by his characteristic stance.

'Washakie . . . he had to come. It important. Wild hoss gone off into desert. It not safe for Washakie or his Indian brothers to go after stallion. Sheriff an' posse might have same idea, an' if they meet up with Indian. . . .'

He ceased on a dramatic gesture, drawing his hand across his throat.

The next moment, the Indian was asking Kirk to go off in search of the horse.

'Him gone off east to the mountains,' Washakie said. 'Mebbe you trail him an' see he gets back to range in north?'

Kirk was astounded at the proposal.

'Why me?'

'You only one who bin good to wild hoss, an' him show no fear of you,' was the quick reply.

55

Kirk remained silent. At the back of his mind a new fear was gathering, fear for Dark Fury's safety. Since he was not with the Indians as he and Burke had supposed earlier, but was alone somewhere in the desert, the chances were that he might fall again into the hands of Unwin and his partners. In fact, this seemed more than likely in the present circumstances, for it was obvious that neither Washakie nor any member of his tribe dare show their faces within fifty miles of the township without being held responsible for the destruction of the circus. Moreover, they would most certainly be charged with horse stealing which, as Kirk knew well, meant but one thing. . . .

Washakie had not exaggerated the gesture he had made. There was only one law in the west for hoss thieves.

'I might try catchin' him,' Kirk said at last, speaking slowly, and trying to sense the Indian's reaction at the suggestion.

'You no do that,' Washakie replied at once. 'Wild hoss not good for saddle. Him best back on home range.'

Although his voice was pitched low, it was somehow compelling. Kirk could not mistake the meaning behind the words, and felt that Washakie was not only concerned about the stallion's safety, but still regarded the animal as important only to the Cœur D'Alenes, and as such, inviolate from all but the red man.

Washakie's next words confirmed this suspicion.

'The Cœur D'Alenes will see you not go unrewarded if you help. When wild hoss back on home range in north, one of my race will seek you out. Washakie give his word to that.'

There was no mistaking the sincerity behind the Indian's tones. The Cœur D'Alene – that dark shadow of a man identifiable only by his peculiar stance – seemed in that moment an even darker shadow, and just as inscrutable. He might have been an arbiter of Destiny – his, Kirk's, and Dark Fury's destinies.

Then Washakie began to speak again, this time in a voice that was almost a monotone, without cadence and without any noticeable break in the sentences that sprang so readily to his lips.

Hope and Faith in the future were clearly his as he described Dark Fury as the special gift the Great Spirit had sent to that distant northland range to bring honour and distinction to the Cœur D'Alenes by the many fine horses he sired. The range and the Lost River Valley were sacred as the stallion's province; his refuge, Lost Canyon itself.

The horse was the elect of the wind; the giver of life to the fleet of foot, the guardian of the solitudes; the black lord of the stone-faced mountain that watched steadfastly over Lost Canyon. He was equal to the eagle as the watcher of the trails ... and these things only because he was free and wild. ...

As he listened, Kirk seemed to witness the great unfurling of an entirely new world – a world he had never known before; and the most important place in that world was Lost Canyon – that fabulous valley of gold.

When at last Washakie had ceased extolling the stallion's many qualities and titles, Kirk knew that he would do exactly as the Indian asked, without caring over much as to the reward he was likely to receive at the end from the Cœur D'Alenes. Sufficient for him would be the knowledge that the end of the trek would have brought him just that much nearer to the fabled Lost Canyon. No man could wish for a greater reward than that.

His next thought put an end to his dreaming. How was he to find the stallion, and even if he succeeded, how was he to find the trail north?

He voiced his fears to Washakie.

'Perhaps it won't be easy to pick up the stallion's trail,' he said.

The Indian shook his head.

'That not difficult,' Washakie replied at once. 'Wild hoss go east from corral. Follow tracks in sand. That easy. Likely sheriff an' bad men will do same at sun-up. You start very early. Take plenty of water. Desert dry. ...'

Then after a short pause, he went on: 'Mebbe at Sun Rock you find wild hoss. Main wash across desert lead to mountain. In red man's day, Piute lived on mountain. ...'

Suddenly the Indian pressed a small object into Kirk's hand, murmuring as he did so: 'This good thing to have. Bring much good luck. Show to Cœur D'Alene when he come an' you get reward. ... Washakie speak truth an' not forget. ...'

Before Kirk was able to question Washakie further, or thank him for the talisman, the Indian had gone, vanishing as quickly as he had appeared. No sound could he hear of Washakie's retreating footsteps, nothing save the memory of his voice saying 'Mebbe at Sun Rock you find wild hoss. . . .'

For a second or two longer he stood listening intently, clutching in a moist palm the small image he had received. Then as once again the glowing embers at his feet flickered into a fitful uprising of flame, he glanced at the thing he held in his hand.

He gave a gasp.

It was a beautifully carved image of a horse, a horse, moreover, black as Dark Fury. He knew then that the stallion was in very truth sacred to the Cœur D'Alenes, and that Washakie in bidding him trail the animal and drive him back to that home range in the north, had entrusted him with a special mission.

Instilled in him then was the disquieting thought that it was not altogether fear of the sheriff and his posse that kept the Indians from trailing the horse themselves. There was something more to it than that. Mebbe they had some other task on hand . . . that of keeping Unwin and his pardners under surveillance. . . . Mebbe too, even with no assistance from one such as he, Dark Fury would eventually find his way back north.

Kirk didn't know what to think. Nevertheless, the uncertainty of his thoughts could not quell the excitement he felt. He was eager to be on the desert trail. He was still in the grip of excitement when he finally made for his caravan, not to sleep, but to plan for the morning.

He had already decided on one thing, and that was to visit Tom Burke a little before sun-up and tell him what he proposed doing. Kirk felt that Burke would readily understand, and even offer him advice. It would perhaps be unwise to mention the visit of Washakie after what had happened, but Kirk felt that he could explain everything just by mentioning his desire to trail the stallion. Mebbe Burke could tell him exactly where Sun Rock was, and whether it had any other significance apart from its ancient associations with the Piutes.

The more he thought about it, gazing repeatedly at the image

Washakie had given him, the more did he long for the night to pass so that he could be on the trail.

He felt, somehow, that Sun Rock might be the stepping stone to Lost Canyon. . . .

Way out on the desert, a lost dog set up a wild lament.

Kirk found himself wondering what had disturbed the animal, and hoped that the stallion was not returning to the scene of his so recent captivity. The lad smiled and shook his head. On second thoughts, he decided that there was little fear of Dark Fury doing that. His hatred of Unwin and his gang would deter him from such a course. Without a doubt, the stallion was far out in the desert by now . . . mebbe following the main wash the Indian had mentioned, and heading direct for Sun Rock. . . .

With a sigh of satisfaction, Kirk stretched himself and yawned, suddenly aware that he was very weary. A few minutes later, he was sleeping soundly, the smile still on his face. At the hour when the night was darkest, with the new day waiting way off on the remote horizons of the east, Kirk began to dream. He seemed to see the vague out-thrust of a pile of rocks, with a blaze of light behind them like the sun at day break. When he finally awoke, there were no rocks to meet his eyes, but there was the uncertain trembling of the dawn advancing across the desert where, when the night was old, a lost dog had howled his distress to the stars, and a stallion had gone racing like the black wind whose name he bore. . . .

Book Two
The Land of Far Horizons

Chapter Seven

Sun rock was all that its name implied – a fantastic outcrop of rock that was never out of the fierce glare of the sun. It rose in buttressed walls of weathered sandstone from out of the floor of the desert. The entire ridge was fashioned after the manner of a gigantic horseshoe, the precipitous cliffs Dark Fury had glimpsed supporting, on closer inspection, the enormous pinnacles and crags which were crumbling away with age. In places, they were so split and broken that it seemed only the slightest of touches was required to bring them crashing down in an avalanche of dust.

Indeed, typical of the desert surrounding it, Sun Rock was nothing but a colourful ruin, sculptured by countless ages of seasonal change that, in the end, would bring it to final destruction.

Ruin, too, had penetrated its very heart. The canyon which thrust deep into it was boulder-strewn and desolate, hemmed in on either side by the leaning cliffs and pinnacled monuments, with no sound to break the deep silence save, in the night watches, the whimpering of the wind in the cave dwellings and tunnels.

A grim enough place, but to Dark Fury, a refuge because of the cool, dark cavern in which he rested, protected from the heat and glare of the pitiless sun. His greatest problem was still the lack of fresh water. Whilst he constantly licked the walls of the cavern for the moisture that gave temporary relief to his tongue, it was not long before he was in a condition worse than before. The moisture that attracted his attention filtered down through rock long since decayed by the desert alkali, and far from relieving the stallion's thirst, made him, after an hour or so, more parched than ever.

At last, he was driven to seek out a possible source of fresh water supply. Despite the fact his nose told him there was none to be had in the vicinity of Sun Rock, on the second day of his sojourn in the cavern, just as the sun was rising, he thrust up into the canyon. It was an eerie enough place in the full blaze of mid-day, but in the half-light of early morning, it possessed a shrunken, grey appearance as if it were as old as time itself.

Awed by the silence of the place, the stallion trod delicately, aware that a false step might send a boulder moving and bring the ancient walls tumbling about him. As he pressed on, his ears aslant against his skull, and his eyes constantly on the alert, the gorge narrowed until he came at last to a pear-shaped pinnacle that concealed a tunnel that struck upwards into the highest of the peaks.

By this time, Dark Fury was convinced that nowhere in that desolation was to be found the one thing he craved most – running water. Yet he tarried for some minutes, sniffing the dry atmosphere, and seeking for a clue as to what might be hidden in the tunnel behind the finger of rock. In his curiosity, he thrust his head around the pillar and tested the air emanating from the cavern.

He sneezed and whistled through his nostrils with disapproval. The almost motionless air was close and stifling as if the very breath of the decaying mountain was concealed in that dark, tortuous corridor.

Only one living thing in that world of monumental rock had witnessed Dark Fury moving up into the dust and ruin of the canyon. That was the feathered god of evil – the vulture! He blinked as he sat watching on his lime-whitened crag, the slow-passing hours meaning nothing to him who had known so many in this awesome place of time-laden decay.

Meanwhile, the sun was once more rising over the eastern confines of the desert, and the western wall of the canyon was attracting a little of the light. The fantastic pinnacles became rose-coloured against the stark blue of the sky; then every detail on the ridge became revealed, each boulder seeming larger than it actually was, each gully being drawn in firm lines that broadened after five hundred feet or so to

61

become a shoot with a spume of debris like a petrified flood one day to be released with violence upon the canyon.

Dark Fury had started to retrace his steps. He walked as one who was again weary, his head lowered and his legs moving slowly and cautiously. He sensed with the uncanny intuition of his kind that if he did not soon leave this canyon of dust, he would die in it.

Whilst on his trek up the canyon he had been grimly aware of the danger that threatened from bulging cliffs, he seemed to be more sensitive than ever on the return trail. More than once he experienced the almost overwhelming desire to suddenly break into a gallop and so make a quick exit from the terrifying gorge. Only the knowledge that here was no place to hightail it as he had done across the desert when he had escaped from captivity, restrained him.

Perhaps it was due to the exceptional care he took to foreshorten his pacing that almost brought him to disaster. He was about halfway down the trail when it happened. He missed a step at a point where the shale was loose and uneven, and stumbling, was brought to his knees.

A broken nicker of pain came from him which, no sooner uttered, changed to a rising scream of terror.

His ears had caught a sound like the beating of mighty wings thundering down from the lime-whitened crag high above him, as the vulture, judging this to be a favourable moment to strike at his prey, came hurtling in to the attack.

The creature's violent passage through the air caused a stream of dust to fly off the terraced ledges, and as he keeled over to make straight for the prostrate stallion, the dust trail seemed to follow him like a foul cloud.

Contrary to the habits of his tribe, this vulture of Sun Rock had learnt from past experiences that instead of waiting for his intended victims to die a slow, lingering death, a decisive attack at the right moment could bring about the end so much quicker. Moreover, such prey which, from time to time, had found its way into death canyon, finally to be harried by the bird, had been so terror-stricken at sight of the vulture planing downwards in attack that it became an easy conquest.

In the case of Dark Fury, however, the vulture had been completely deceived by the stallion's dejected appearance and fall, and was taken by surprise when the horse suddenly leapt to his feet and reared on hind legs to beat off the attack.

As the stallion's wild scream of fury echoed through the gorge, the bird tried to check his downward thrust.

Unfortunately, for him, there was no movement of air in the canyon, and the creature's attempt to break his flight was clumsy in execution. Dark Fury's sudden leap upward with threshing hooves did, by the very nature of this formidable line of defence, give the vulture a presentiment of danger which forced him into a halfroll that carried him off his course.

He uttered a savage shriek and beat his way along the ravine, turning abruptly and coming in low to renew his attack on the horse.

Dark Fury had recovered somewhat from his fall and the fright. Now in full possession of his faculties, all the inherent cunning of his kind came into play to circumvent the new assault the bird essayed to make.

He plunged forward, and again the vulture was taken by surprise. This time, his line of flight was even more hazardous. Before he could bring his wings into movement and rise to a sufficient height to avoid impact with the stallion, Dark Fury was on him.

Once again he gave a raucous shriek, and only by a dexterous side-spin did he avoid serious harm. One pinion, none the less, received damage from Dark Fury's ploughing hooves, and the bird was hard put to beat upwards safely.

Fully roused, the stallion thought only of revenge. The sense of caution that had previously dominated his actions, making him move slowly along the floor of the canyon, disappeared with his mounting tide of fury. Despite the tribulations he had undergone, his anger made him once again what he had been in that distant valley of the lost rivers – a wild stallion who was leader of the herd.

He swung about savagely and leaped upwards, all the while screaming as he watched his late enemy climbing away beyond reach of his hooves. Then once more his feet slipped on the loosened shale, and in endeavouring to keep his balance, he collided with an insecure boulder.

In the moment that the harassed vulture reached his roosting crag, a ponderous rumbling rolled upwards from the floor of the canyon, accompanied by a swirl of dust that gathered in intensity as the rumbling increased.

The entire canyon was a seething cloud of acrid dust, accompanied by the increasing vibration of sound that echoed from cliff to cliff as the boulder which Dark Fury had set into motion rolled on its way, setting up a series of small avalanches which, in turn, started to bring the rotten pinnacles crashing down.

No pent-up fury of an electric storm could have possessed such violence. It was a rising sound that pealed, roared and whistled; and before it, wild-eyed and racing as he had never raced before, was Dark Fury.

He had almost reached the entrance to the outer world when one of the largest of the pinnacles came toppling down, bringing with it part of the ridge that just sank towards the floor of the canyon in a deepening cloud of dust that went rolling upwards to finally spread like an enormous mushroom over the summit of the entire range.

Terror of the destruction taking place between the crashing walls of rock gave the horse a turn of speed and strength of purpose such as he had never possessed before, not even in his finest moments. As boulder after boulder came crashing and tossing after him, and the débris of a million years or more showered the trail behind him, he stretched his body to its utmost limits as he sped nearer and nearer to that gap in the mountain wall leading to safety. . . .

At last he was through – the mocking sound of the avalanche pursuing him as he continued to race far out into the desert, halting only when he had reached the comparative security of the dwarfed cedars that had the appearance of being tossed and shaken by a cyclone that was bodiless and without movement.

Breathless, Dark Fury stood gazing back.

The rumbling as of heavy thunderclaps still echoed from the heart of the range, and the dust still continued to rise. Soaring high over it all was the shape of the vulture, wheeling and turning and shrieking angrily as he witnessed the destruction that was changing the entire course of death canyon.

When evening finally came, with a few wisps of cloud unfurling like crimson claws in the west, the pall of dust still hung over Sun Rock, but the vulture was no longer visible, nor yet Dark Fury.

The mountain was now a completely deserted ruin!

Chapter Eight

The lost dog out in the desert had again started his wild lament as Kirk Merrett left his wagon in the grey light of the dawn and made for the more elaborate caravan in which Tom Burke slept. It did not occur to him that the circus proprietor might still be asleep. He only knew that he was filled with a great unrest, and eager to be on his way.

Burke, however, was very much awake when Kirk knocked at the wagon door. In fact, he had not slept at all during the night, but once, about three in the morning, had gone outside to view the remains of the fire. It was then that he had seen Luke Unwin and his three henchmen returning from the saloon. They were talking loudly as they approached the showground, and Enos Wills, who had apparently only just joined up with the others, was speaking of an Indian who had remained behind when the others had made a hasty departure.

Keeping well back in the shadows, Burke heard Wills say that the Indian was much concerned because Dark Fury had broken free and was out in the desert.

Unwin had remarked that after sun-up they must all set off and trail the animal.

Wills and the others were all for letting Dark Fury go.

'Them Indians will be after him too,' Wills had remarked significantly. 'That is if they can keep clear of the sheriff.'

Unwin had laughed at that.

'We'll jest heve to see to it that they can't,' he said. 'Mebbe we'll take the sheriff along with us . . . jest fer the ride. . . .'

All four men then turned towards their wagons, the last remark Burke heard being concerned with Wills' absence from the circus.

'That feller who wuz out gunnin' fer yez sure meant business if he set eyes on yez,' Bill Maitland said, as he and Corson made for their own particular van.

'You did well in hidin' out on him,' Unwin was heard to remark as he clambered up the steps of the wagon he shared with Wills.

Not many second later Burke was able to come from out of the shadow, waiting for a few minutes until all sound of movement from both wagons assured him that the men had finally bunked down.

He had decided to speak to Kirk about the matter first thing in the morning, and was still pondering over the mystery of the stallion when Kirk Merrett knocked at the wagon door.

Burke listened patiently to all the young fellow had to say, then proceeded to tell him what he himself had overheard.

'Seems to me that if you want to get on to that hoss fust, you'd better be hittin' the trail,' he said.

There was a queer smile on his face as he spoke.

He was regarding Kirk through half-closed eyes. There was a sudden quickening of his heart as he recalled, almost poignantly now, some forgotten memory of his own youth, particularly that part of it bound up with thoroughbred horses in his native Ireland. How like Kirk he had been in those far-off days! Indeed, as he looked at the lad, he thought he could discern in his eyes a hint of that same excitement that had sent him as a young man hastening off to a new untried country in search of adventure.

Maybe something of his youth was alive in him yet, urging him to give Kirk every encouragement, and before he knew it, he was telling the lad to be on his way, taking with him two of the circus mustangs.

'You'll be needin' an extra hoss to carry yeer packs,' he explained, and then proceeded to tell him what little he knew of Sun Rock. 'It's four, mebbe five day's trek out into the desert,' he said. 'You'll have to take plenty water. There's none this side o' the Big Lake Mountains, an' sonny, believe me, they're a heck o' a way off.'

Kirk thanked him as best he could, suddenly aware that Burke for all his brusque manner had a real heart beneath that fancy waistcoat of his, and what was more, still had a spark of adventure left in him.

Burke then paid Kirk off, giving him a deal more money than was actually due to him, and saying that when he was through trailing the stallion, he could come back to the circus life whenever he wished.

'You'll find me aisy enough, me boyo,' he added. 'Sure, it's a grander circus I'll be havin' from this out. I'll be hittin' the trail west in a few days, an' 'll be some place in Nevada should you want to join up with me.'

He held out his hand.

Kirk grasped it firmly.

'You're a great guy.' Kirk's voice was husky.

Burke laughed and shrugged his shoulders.

'Goodbye now,' he remarked, 'an' good luck to ye. . . .'

Kirk sensed the showman's embarrassment, and with another handshake, left the caravan.

An hour later, with the sun now well above the horizon, Kirk left the showground with two of Burke's best horses. To avoid rousing the suspicions of anybody who might see him, he set off westwards as if bound for the Nevada State line. When he finally turned about to make for the desert, he did so from a northerly direction.

He was more than an hour on the trail before he picked up Dark Fury's hoof marks. He was trembling with excitement as he dismounted to examine them the more closely. There was not the slightest doubt that they belonged to the stallion. They were large and deeply set as if the creature who had made them was travelling fast, and pounding the trail heavily in his anxiety to escape possible pursuit.

The sharp thought of pursuit made Kirk glance hurriedly back along the desert track. All he could see was the unending vista of sand and whale-back dunes. Apparently, Luke Unwin and his pardners were sleeping late, or else were confident that they could pick up the stallion's trail without effort when they were ready to set off.

Kirk remounted and hoping to confuse them, did his utmost to obliterate Dark Fury's imprints by keeping his own horses treading over them. Thus, behind him was the blurred impression of hooves clearly not those of one horse, but two, while ahead, keeping to the main wash, the imprints of Dark Fury went on and on ... leading Kirk knew not where, but none the less, leading to a place where, in time, he would assuredly be found.

As he rode on following the stallion's track, despite the heat, Kirk considered it was all certainly well worth the trouble.

Somewhere ... at the end of the trail ... was Lost Canyon!

Moving as quickly as was consistent with his regard for his horses, Kirk put a distance of some twenty miles behind him before deciding to take a much-needed rest. The going had been more difficult than he had anticipated; the heat very oppressive.

He selected for his first camp a spot where a high ridge afforded a little shade, and here he watered the animals from the supply he carried, and gave them both a small sprinkling of dried grass which, at the last moment, he had thrust into two medium-sized sacks. He then spread a saddle blanket on the sand and ate a little food himself.

Kirk knew that he could not take his ease for long. That warning of Burke's could not be ignored. .... 'Sun Rock ... it's four, mebbe five days' trek into the desert. . . .'

The question of water was going to be his greatest problem if, by chance, he lost the way and took an extra couple of days to reach the rock. Since he understood also that there was no water to be had at Sun Rock, he would have to search for the nearest water-hole within a day, at the most, of reaching the locality.

With this thought uppermost in his mind, immediately he had finished eating, Kirk climbed out of the depression of the wash and standing on the ridge, stared back along the trail. No sign of life could he see.

He then turned and looked east. The same barren undulating sameness met his eyes ... an immense wilderness of sand that seemed to flow on and on to that distant line of hills which he sensed must be the Big Lake Mountains Burke spoke about.

A few minutes later, he had saddled up and was once again on the trail.

For the whole of that day he pressed on, following the main wash already traversed by Dark Fury. It was fast approaching sunset when Kirk started to seek out a small hollow in which to set up his second camp. His eyes ached from the continual glare of the sun, and for the first time in his life, he felt sore with riding so long without a break.

The entire floor of the desert appeared to be changing before his eyes. The yellow changed to bronze, the bronze to crimson as the westering sun sank towards the far off canyons of Nevada. Soon it would be dusk.

At last he found what seemed to be a likely place in which to set up camp. He took saddles and packs from the horses, and again watering and feeding them, set about attending to his own wants. First he set up a rough and ready type of tent, then after digging down into the sand, managed to find sufficient decayed stalks of what had once been cactus and mesquite, and from them, kindled a small fire over which he cooked his supper.

The dusk deepened; stars began to shine brightly above, the largest being those low down on the horizon. Even as he watched, he could see the last of the day reluctantly flickering and dying away in the west.

Leaning forward, Kirk stirred the fire into a stronger resemblance of a blaze, and sat for a long time huddled over it. He was not exactly cold, but he was aware of a chill inside him ... a chill, moreover, that gripped him the more tenaciously whenever he thought of Dark Fury, lost, as he felt, in this treeless waste that stretched monotonously from the Nevada State line to that of Colorado.

Little by little the black arc of the darkness encroached on the camp, closed down upon the two horses, then upon Kirk himself. The fire died in its ashes. The stars way up above shone brighter than ever.

Lying stretched out on his blanket, Kirk watched them, conscious of the utter loneliness of the desert, the ever present sense of remoteness because life, under such hazardous conditions, was such a fragile thing, dependent on so little, and yet upon so much.

As his eyes closed in sleep, Kirk was about to question the future he might have in that uncertain span of life. He was already framing the words in his mind, then the problem no longer troubled him. It was gone, smoothed away by the invisible hand that pressed lightly upon his eyelids bringing him without effort to the deep, fathomless darkness that was the darkness of sleep that allowed for no outward ripple to disturb its brief moment of oblivion.

Late though the hour was when Kirk fell into that unbroken slumber, he was yet awake quite early, when the grey gloom still made it difficult to pick out any salient features of the desert.

After a hasty breakfast, he broke camp, and day was just beginning to take on a definite shape when he set out on the trail again.

He rode hard for some hours, still keeping to the main wash, and following those clearly defined footprints. The heat seemed worse than before, and the desert more than ever an expanse of featureless sand that led to what could only be described as no definite horizon.

Every feeling Kirk experienced became more intense as the long hours wore on and his discomfort from the heat increased. Nevertheless, he never once faltered in his resolve to keep hard on the trail. Somewhere, at the end of it, was the one creature he sought ... Dark Fury!

Thus, three more days and nights did he spend in this desert journeying, days which took him farther and farther away from civilisation such as was understood by the folk who inhabited the Mormon township, and nights which, by their very silence, brought sleep instantaneously to eyes grown tired with so much gazing upon endless miles of sand in which the impress of a stallion's footmarks told of an adventure only just begun.

From then on, Kirk seemed to lose all touch with time. He just kept doggedly on the trail, sleeping only when dusk came, and starting off again immediately it was light.

It was late on what had been a particularly tiring afternoon when he struck the thin sprinkling of sage beyond which grew the stunted cacti and mesquite. Although there were still a few hours of daylight remaining, Kirk decided to set up camp. He felt at last the exhaustion such a journey was bound to bring, and knew that he just could not press on further without taking a long rest first.

He set the horses loose where a patch of sage seemed most promising, hobbling them with strips of hide lest they strayed during the night. He then spread out his saddle blanket and succeeded in kindling a good fire. As he looked around, he knew that he need not be sparing with the dead wood. There was more than sufficient amongst the mesquite.

It was the most luxurious evening he had yet spent. With the comforting glow of firelight at his feet, he was able to relax while the sun burnt itself out below the western skyline, and the dusk of another tranquil night brought purple shadow to the desert and an unwavering gloom to the cacti and the dwarfed shrubs.

The horses too appeared quiet and contented. They did not go far from the sageland, and by nightfall, were both dozing, lying down amongst the dry brush instead of standing up as had been their habit in the desert.

Kirk slept long, and soundly. The night was gone and a new day striding up the sky when he was roused by the movement of the horses amongst the sage. He lay still and listened, conscious that for once he was reasonably contented, and did not wish to leave the blanket which he had rolled about himself in so comforting a manner.

He closed his eyes for a further few moments, wallowing in the luxury of the blanket. He thought he heard a mocking bird calling somewhere in the dwarfed shrubland ... maybe, too, the faint twittering of a quail.

Suddenly he was lying taut. ...

No longer was he imagining in the depths of his mind the note of the mocking bird or the distant calling of a quail. There was something more definite in his ears now.

He opened his eyes and stared upwards. The sun was up over the scrubland of cacti and mesquite ... a sun that, for one moment, was glowing red like a ball of fire. Then it seemed to quiver and grow dim, its light fading over the undulating sage ridge where the two horses appeared to be standing in a state of terror, their heads turned to the east. ...

A moment later Kirk's ears held firmly the sound that was reaching out towards him from the east ... a slow rumbling that seemed to shake the very earth beneath him . . . an awesome sound that went on and on . . . deep . . . thundering . . . echoing . . . fading. . . .

As he struggled out of his blanket, the horses, badly startled, came stumbling in his direction

By the time they had reached him, the rumbling was no longer heard, but a cloud seemed to lie betwixt the desert and the sun . . . a cloud that grew until it resembled a storm gathering in the uncharted airways of the sky. . . .

Chapter Nine

For almost an hour after the terrifying avalanche in the canyon of Sun Rock, Dark Fury stood within the shelter of the forest of cedar. The trees were no longer shaken by that deep subterranean force, but were motionless like the stallion who stood amongst them.

Soon after reaching the forest, the animal had suffered an incomprehensible attack of fright, and for quite a while had been powerless to move a limb before him. That ordeal in the canyon was something he would never forget despite the fact that he had escaped injury from the falling rocks.

It was not until the huge dust cloud over Sun Rock had thinned away in the upper reaches of the air that he regained a little of his habitual calm. Even then, his eyes did not cease from watching the ominous shape that continued to hover high over the desolation of the canyon, searching in vain for the pinnacle that had long been its roosting place.

With the dispersal of the dust cloud, however, the sunlight began to shine brightly upon the wrecked walls of the mountain. Only the gap leading to the canyon remained in heavy shadow, the shadow continuing far into that desolation of boulder and debris where loose stones still fell rattling from insecure ledges and a thin powdering of dust drifted, caught by straying currents of air.

Round about high noon, the vulture planed down, coming to rest on a boulder that was split in half by its impact with the canyon floor.

The bird sat hunched in its feathers. More than ever did it appear to be the very embodiment of evil.

With the departure of the vulture, Dark Fury started to move amongst the cedars, searching the sage for something moist to ease the thirst that was tormenting him. After a while, he stood close to one of the trees and waited for the sun to go down. He knew that he would have to set off immediately it was dusk. Fresh water was now a most pressing necessity.

The approach of evening over the ruined face of Sun Rock was a melancholy spectacle. With the sudden glowing of the sunset, the splintering towers held for a brief moment the warmth of those westering fires. As they faded, there was left only the purpling gloom that lined every gully until the entire rock reared dark and barren like the shell of an uprising crater, devoid of all beauty, and about to disappear for ever in the darkness that came billowing up behind it.

There seemed to be no discernible pause in the departure of the day and the coming of night to the neighbourhood of the rock. One moment the huge edifice was still visible; then it was gone ... completely swallowed up, leaving in its place a sense of the magnitude of the earth and the utter inscrutableness of Nature.

In all that brooding immensity, Dark Fury and the unsleeping vulture in the canyon were the only living atoms.... Everything else was dead!

With the sudden falling of the darkness, a sense of orientation came to the stallion, an orientation stronger than anything he had yet encountered. Since his greatest need was for water, his widely flaring nostrils sought for some trace of it in every veering current of air, and suddenly he knew the actual direction he must take.

His head went up and he faced the north. There was a strong current of air reaching out into the desert, moving amidst the cedars; and it was air that held the unmistakable taint of moisture ... moisture from far in the north where the Raft River Mountain looked out over the State boundary line to the fertile valleys of Idaho. No salt deserts there; no scent of decay and desolation .... Only the lushness of land well watered and timbered ... the land the stallion once knew as home.

No uncertainty was in him then as he sniffed that drift of air from the north, no necessity for a trail beneath his feet to lead him hence. He knew without a vestige of a doubt that he must travel due north ... away from the ruin of Sun Rock and the ancient track that had led him across the desert from his place of captivity.

The wind – that ally of all wild things – had come to tell him of that which was his inheritance. What it did not tell him was that many miles of desert still lay between him and the coveted water ... miles that were as arid as any he had yet encompassed, miles that would tax his remaining strength and seek to destroy him.

Perhaps the great Spirit of Fur and Hide that guided all such as Dark Fury was standing way out in the gloom at the moment when the stallion decided to start off at once. Perhaps because Dark Fury was so much a part of the wild, that same Spirit brought from out of the north a stronger current of air so that the horse ran into it without discomfort ... and so continued to run until the night was no more and another day, wan like the desert he was traversing, stood away off in the east fluttering its coloured streamers into the very maw of the sun.

Those few short hours of darkness had seen Dark Fury put more than twenty miles behind him so that when the sun was well up over the horizon, the fateful rock was little more than a knuckle rising up from the floor of the desert.

As he pressed on, the desert became broken in places by clumps of wind-shapen shrub and seamed with enormous ridges that ran from north to south as if fashioned by heavy flows of water in the centuries that had gone.

Yet no moisture lay in the adjacent water-holes now – nothing but sand and the bleached remains of long dead brushwood.

A little before noon, Dark Fury had run himself to a halt. For the past hour or more, his running had been purely an effort to escape from the torment of thirst, and when at last he was forced to stop, he staggered from weakness, his sides heaving and a thin rope of saliva hanging from his muzzle. Once again his head drooped between his shoulders, and his eyes, blood-shot from the constant exposure to sand and heat, closed wearily.

His strength was fast running out.

Through those few short hours of darkness, he had no more than pursued an unidentified trail, driven onwards by some deep-rooted urge. No longer was there any current of air from the north to sustain him with the promise of water. Even as he stood swaying on his legs with his head drooping miserably, as if to torment him still further, there seemed to be moving through him a slow procession of phantoms ... phantoms that came from canyons and valleys where was water ... running water cold as ice. ...

Dark Fury shook himself as if to keep his senses alert.

The phantoms continued their steady journey through the dark passages of his mind ... a serried array of wild horses and other creatures he had known, all passing and re-passing along those trails the stallion remembered from his colt-hood days. There was a strange twilight and dusk upon those trails now, and upon the shadows that passed along them; but there was no twilight and certainly no dusk upon the winged shape that suddenly appeared high overhead, turning slowly in the sky on outstretched pinions.

Dark Fury gave a heavy sigh and awakened from his tormented moment of rest. Then he stumbled and started to sink to his knees ... tired ... almost prepared to give up the struggle.

Seeing the stallion thus beset with weakness, the vulture once again essayed a manoeuvre to strike him down, and this time completely destroy the prey he had pursued since daybreak; and once again was the vicious creature's judgement at fault. He was over-optimistic, and failed to recognise a will as savage as his own.

For the first time in many days, a cloud was unfurling in the sky ... a thin wisp of a thing; and through it came the vulture, hurtling down upon the stallion.

A sound, reminiscent of an event that had almost brought him to disaster, must have reached Dark Fury's ears, despite his weariness and overwhelming desire to sleep. Like a flash, he reared up, whirling around with head set high and eyes searching the skies.

Swiftly the vulture came at him, falling earthwards like a winged thunder-bolt, and, as on the previous occasion, the bird was travelling much too quickly to break that death-dealing stoop. Even as he endeavoured to flatten out, so did Dark Fury move into action, at first snaking away then leaping upwards as if on springs, uttering as he did so a brassy, whinnying scream.

Balancing himself on his hind legs, he used his forelegs and hooves to advantage, cleaving the air with each stroke and suddenly catching his enemy who was attempting an upward sweep.

The instant his hooves encountered the feathered shape, the stallion became a living tornado. He leapt and whirled with such a savage intensity of movement that had the bird completely at his mercy, and when at last the shrieking creature fell beneath those threshing feet, the pounding on the body went on for some minutes until nothing remained but a shapeless mass of feathers that bore no resemblance whatever to the living thing they once had been.

His mental awareness of the danger that had threatened him brought all his unsuspected reserves of energy into play once again.

In a moment, he became once more a creature of great stamina and purpose. The torment of thirst was temporarily forgotten as he sought to put as much distance as was possible between himself and the lifeless mass at his feet. Here, in the desert, there was no danger from falling rocks as in that canyon at Sun Rock. His body became stretched to its greatest extent as he raced like the wind from the scene of the vulture's inglorious defeat, and he did not slacken his pace until exhaustion once again forced him to stop.

This time, he stumbled to his knees the very instant he ceased running, and lay for more than a couple of hours like a creature that would never more rise to his feet.

Dark Fury, however, came from a long line of stallions who had never known man as their master, and who, from great privation in the wild, were quick to recuperate under the most hazardous of conditions.

Thus, by sundown, the stallion experienced the swift surging of blood once again through his veins. His head went up slowly as he felt the heat of day departing from the skies above him, and despite his parched throat, all the old eager interest to renew the desperate struggle welled up in him like a strong, returning tide.

Some vague memory of Kirk was in it, a memory of the lad bringing him water, followed by yet another memory, a little less clear in his mind, of the lad struggling with those who were ill-treating him.

Dark Fury regained his feet after an effort, and his bloodshot eyes gazed longingly towards the north where he knew he would find water if he could but force himself to complete the long journey across the desert. Then, as once before when he was nigh to being beaten, a strong current of wind came from out of that northland of high hills; and again did it bring him the unmistakable taint of water.

A frantic eagerness to be on his way caused his limbs to quiver as he sniffed the scent of water carried so strongly to him in the wind. His ears twitched a little. His bloodshot eyes seemed to glow brightly. It wasn't only the nature of the horse in him that rebelled against dying alone here in the desert; it was those countless other stallions from whom he had sprung who refused to let him give up. They, too, had endured what Dark Fury was now enduring, and because they had triumphed against adversity, they sought to do so again by bringing spurts of strength to the rising turbulence of Dark Fury's blood.

Before the sun had departed behind the last desert ridge, Dark Fury was off once more, not racing any longer, but moving at an easy pace that carried him over the desert without undue strain. As he forged steadily on, so did the day die out over the featureless continent of sand, and night came with its myriad stars, all twinkling brightly like lanterns lit in the arc of the infinite.

Hour after hour, the stallion kept at his easy trotting, and hour after hour the wind kept coming at him, urging him on.

The night was almost spent when Dark Fury's feet encountered sagebrush once more, and then as the dawn came up, he found that he was approaching an undulating plain of greasewood bounded in the north-west by the distant shapes of hills.

By now his pace was becoming slower. Nevertheless, he continued to struggle on. It was not until the sun was well up that he could see clearly the line of hills that lay directly ahead, and saw that the opposing cliffs were broken by innumerable canyons. He could also glimpse what seemed to be a mass of dwarf cedars growing amidst a scattering of boulders spilled down from the heights above.

Stumbling on, the stallion knew now that he had not been misled by that taint in the wind. The smell of the water was almost a taste on his parched tongue.

The hours continued to fall one by one from the pattern of light that made up the long day; high noon came and went; the afternoon grew wan and another night stood away off in the east.

It was as the sun went down in dying flame in the west that Dark Fury, scarcely aware of moving any longer, came at last to a deep wash filled with reddish water. His eyes no longer saw the nearby line of cliffs and the dwarf cedars; nor did his ears pick up the sounds habitual to this outpost of the mountains of Idaho.

He saw only the red glow of the water, and heard nothing but the pounding of his own heart that seemed to shake the whole of his tortured body.

Without hesitation, he made straight for the wash, stumbling, almost without control over his limbs, into the quaking mass that seeped away into the water. At last he felt the water rising up to his fetlocks ... then to his knees, and shuddering violently, he only knew that he was standing up to his flanks in it, and that he was drinking ... drinking. ...

The water darkened as he moved farther and farther into it ... the sand gripped his feet ... gripped and squeezed. ... Almost too late did he realise that he was held in quicksands ... almost too late the effort he made to fight his way back to safe ground. He screamed with rising terror ... screamed and threshed and struggled against the pull of the sand. ...

Then as the last of the day flickered and went out, he succeeded in dragging himself half out of the swamp before collapsing.

An hour later, he lay completely motionless save for his heavy breathing.

Over the swamp was a haze; the dark water was but a burnished mirror of rust that dimly reflected the countless stars that glowed high above it.

Chapter Ten

On that last evening he spent brooding on the crag in the canyon of Sun Rock, the vulture had no premonition of the violent end that was to come to him; indeed, in his brooding, the evil creature was aware only of the destruction he hoped to bring to the stallion. All through that last night he was to know, the bird kept waking, and, as the last hour of darkness drew away from the edge of the world, he preened his feathers and kept glancing up at the ruined walls about him, waiting for the first glimpse of sunrise to break the gloom.

One other too was watching for the first sign of dawn that morning. That was Kirk Merrett who, the previous evening, had set up camp in the small forest of cedar. He was anxious to examine the fantastic mountain pile that lay so short a distance from the dwarf timber, and was hoping that perhaps somewhere, amidst those broken rocks, he would find some evidence of Dark Fury. The canyon, which he had seen the following night just as the sun went down, was the first place he intended exploring. If anything, it was there he hoped to find the stallion.

The ruined aspect of the range, whilst telling of the numerous falls of rock that had brought about its shattered appearance, did not altogether tell of the sudden ruin that had taken place in the canyon, and Kirk, as yet, did not quite connect that mysterious rumbling he had heard way back in the desert with an event associated with Sun Rock itself.

He had already saddled up when the dawn came like a leaping

tongue of flame from out of the east, and Kirk had just mounted when he was held spellbound by the sight of the vulture thrusting up into the air. The huge bird seemed to rise from some hidden place deep in the heart of the range, and had the appearance of being in great haste which, in fact, he was, for he had suddenly realised that Dark Fury had made his escape under cover of the darkness. Even on the first turn he made over the shattered pinnacles of the range, he glimpsed Kirk Merrett and the two horses standing where, but a few short hours before, he had seen Dark Fury.

Without a sound, he went flying over the serrated ridge of Sun Rock, flapping clumsily as he sought out a spiral of air likely to aid him to soar to a height from which he could extend his vision and glimpse whatever movement there might be in the desert.

Kirk, sitting at ease in the saddle, watched the bird closely. It required no specialised knowledge on his part to realise that the creature was searching for something that had clearly commanded his attention the previous evening; and since Kirk was already aware that the stallion's footprints led direct to this place, and continued on in the direction of Sun Rock, he had no difficulty in arriving at the conclusion that the animal the bird craved to see was none other than Dark Fury.

For ten minutes or more, Kirk sat motionless on his horse, watching every movement the vulture made. At last, the bird seemed to encounter the steady stream of air he sought, and in a moment, was soaring rapidly. Up and up he went until he was but a pinioned speck in the blue haze of the sky. Then he went sailing slowly due north, moving away from the area of Sun Rock.

Kirk, interpreting the bird's glide northwards as particularly significant, decided to reduce to a minimum his exploration of the canyon, and continued to mark the vulture's progress northwards until he could see him no longer.

In less than an hour, Kirk, having made a preliminary survey of the cliffs of Sun Rock, prepared to enter the canyon. He tethered his horses amidst a pile of boulders that would afford them ample protection should the vulture suddenly put in an appearance and startle them.

He then proceeded up the acclivity, aware of the ring of his footsteps on the broken rock, and dubiously glancing upwards at the towering cliffs which, at one point, seemed to completely overhang the narrow defile. Five minutes later, he was in the canyon.

The desolation appalled him. At last he understood the reason for the ominous rumble he had heard the previous morning. There was no mistaking the recent fall of rock. Many of the boulders were even now insecurely lodged and it would not take much to set off another devastating avalanche.

He pressed on carefully.

Very few signs were left to show where Dark Fury had trod, but here and there he did notice the impress of the stallion's hooves, and at one place, some scattered feathers.

Kirk paused for a moment examining the spot. No clue, however, did he find likely to help him construct what had happened to produce those few broken feathers. He could only surmise that the vulture, for the feathers were clearly those of such a bird, had startled the horse into a display of acrobatics. Whatever else might have happened was beyond his comprehension. He did not even consider the possibility of the event bringing about the avalanche that had so completely changed the floor of the canyon and its opposing cliffs.

At last Kirk stood before the uprising finger of rock keeping guard over the tunnel that thrust upwards into the very bowels of the mountain. Here again he could see the hoof marks, even the scattering of the broken shale where Dark Fury had turned about prior to retracing his steps.

More out of curiosity than anything else, Kirk spent fully fifteen minutes investigating the approaches to the tunnel. The foul air deterred him from entering. Nevertheless, he soon discovered what Dark Fury had known within a few seconds of entering the canyon. The place was as dry as a bleached bone.

Not long afterwards Kirk was on his way back, wondering as he went on the marvels of nature.

The canyon was the strangest place he had ever seen.

He had all but reached the narrow cleft leading to the exit when he paused, staring back. From somewhere in the mountain a curious sound was rising ... a shrill whistling it seemed at first, changing gradually to a more sonorous note.

Then he saw what seemed to be thin streams of dust funnelling out of the caves high up on the broken ledges.

Kirk felt the cold hand of fear clutch his heart, holding him rooted to the spot.

All the old tales he had heard from time to time, most of them dealing with the ancient rites of the Indians, came back to him then. He knew this place to have been one of the last strongholds of the Piutes; he knew too that somewhere hereabouts was the reputed site of their ancient burial caves which, according to legend, if disturbed brought destruction upon the invader.

The whistling from deep within the mountain went on, accompanied by distant rumblings similar to those he had heard way back in the desert. Then one or two small stones came bouncing down from off the ledges high above him, and the streams of dust issuing from the caves seemed to be increasing in density.

Suddenly it all ceased. The last of the dust streams went thinning away until there was no dust left ... and no noises. There was just a deep, impressive silence brooding over the canyon. The inward decay of the mountain was no longer apparent.

For quite a while longer Kirk remained staring back along the canyon. Whilst the sense of fear had gone from him, he yet could not bring himself to leave this strange place of rotting rock and desolation. It was the desolation, more than anything else, that made him reluctant to leave. He knew that he would never see this place again, and sensed deep down inside him that here the hand of time long past had drawn a tracery on the stones and cliffs that was the history of the ancient race that had once dwelt on the mountain. Coupled with that feeling was yet another ... a stronger, more insistent feeling. The past was past indeed, and time now present was striving hard to obliterate what had been so that in the years to come, nothing remained to tell of the rites and ceremonies that had taken place here in the canyon of Sun Rock.

So final was the feeling he experienced that he would have been exceedingly surprised had the vulture suddenly returned to what

Kirk knew had been his home. It was almost as if the bird also had been rejected, and would never more return.

Kirk shuddered, and for a brief instant he felt as if the ancient Piutes were gathered there on the ledges high above him. He could surely see the lazy spiral of a smoke signal, and then realised that it was another stream of dust issuing from yet another cave.

The spell of the canyon was broken at sight of this further warning of danger. Kirk hurried from the spot, relieved at not finding Dark Fury in the canyon. He felt that it would never have been possible to round up the animal in such a place without bringing the entire mountain down.

An hour later, after a short meal, Kirk was again on the trek, pursuing the old tell-tale footprints, and guided as to his ultimate destination by the route taken by the vulture whom, he guessed, was also after the stallion.

Kirk had no fear that the bird would do the stallion harm. He still saw Dark Fury as a spirited creature who could subdue almost anything, and was moreover encouraged by the knowledge that he could not be more than a few hours away from the horse.

He little guessed what lay beyond the distant horizon!

As he rode on in the heat of the day, sitting easily in the saddle like a man who had been wandering the desert trails all his life, his thoughts were no longer concerned with the mystery of the canyon he had left behind him, but with the possible whereabouts of Luke Unwin and his partners. It was queer he had not seen anything of them. Despite the efforts he had taken to obliterate Dark Fury's footprints in the desert immediately adjoining the township, he had felt certain that one or other of the men would have attempted trailing him if only to ascertain his reason for trekking out into the desert. Whilst Kirk was positive they would never have picked out Dark Fury's imprints from amongst those of his own horses, such as were discernible would easily have set them guessing.

There was, of course, one other possibility to be considered. Mebbe, they had gone off north ... to that spot where they had first seen the horse, presuming that sooner or later he would turn up in what was considered his home territory. Such being the case, Kirk felt reasonably sure that Washakie himself, or some other member of the Cœur D'Alene tribe, would be awaiting them.

Even in his own particular case, apart from the promise Washakie had given him, Kirk was absolutely certain that no matter where he went in search of the stallion, whether north, south, east or west, at the end of the trail, he would find the Indian.

Thus backwards and forwards swung the pendulum of his thoughts as his horses picked their way leisurely across the sand. Indeed, many were the things he thought about as he sat comfortably in the saddle, never uttering a single word to the horse, but letting the animal have his head while the pack horse followed sedately in the rear.

Then, almost like an act of betrayal reminding him ruthlessly that he was thirsty, his thoughts began to hover around the question of water in much the same fashion as Dark Fury's had done. Sometimes it was a river he imagined, bubbling up from some subterranean spring, then suddenly booming between the high walls of a canyon. Sometimes it was a lake he saw, wide and deep, then just a stream, trickling away in a watercourse that temptingly followed a trail he once knew.

From water, because he was hot and dusty, there came the faint remembrance of winds he had known, blowing fresh and cool against his face, carrying a strange burden of things where the heat was not so intense. . . .

Kirk suddenly sat up straight in the saddle. For a moment there was the sharp tug of excitement at his heart. There was indeed a breeze flying past him, coming straight from out of the northland.

He sniffed it anxiously, but before he could determine what faint scent it contained, it had gone . . . a mere puff of a breeze that might have come from the cottonwoods or from some other desert.

Kirk began to experience fear. If there was no end to this desert and he did not strike fresh water soon, he and his horses would be in dire distress. The water-bottles and leathern bags were sadly depleted.

He caught his breath with anxiety as he leant over the saddle to stare once again at the imprints he was following. He felt a trifle reassured, for each impression was set firm and deep as if the stallion who had gone before was travelling a direct line north.

Dark Fury seemed to be in no doubt as to what lay at the end of the trail.

Yet in the very moment when he felt that reassurance spring up in him, deep down there was a curious uneasiness. Supposing, after all, neither Dark Fury nor he found water? A couple of days hence and he would be really up against it, and then whether he caught up with the stallion or not, it would not matter much either way. His bones and also the bones of his two horses would be left to bleach in this desert of no known trails.

The very intensity of his thoughts caused Kirk to loosen his coloured neckerchief and peer ahead with a look of anxiety in his eyes. He began to think of the little water that was left in the bottles and the leathern saddle bags . . . enough perhaps for a couple of days, with care . . . certainly not enough for three days.

Once again he straightened up in the saddle. He shook himself awake. Why this lazy passage across the desert? Time was short . . . too short to be comfortable. The pace had to be quickened.

'Gitte up there,' he shouted abruptly.

He spurred his mount to a sharp trot, and was gratified to hear the pack animal also quicken his pace.

So far so good. He only wished the afternoon was not so long in fading. The sun seemed hotter than ever and his need for water was increasing with each mile that passed. He sighed wearily, longing as never before for the cool of an evening breeze, with the sun gone and only the night sky gathering above. Then before he was actually aware of it happening, the day did indeed start to fade, very faintly at first as the sun went down in a shimmering haze that sent diffused rivers of colour pouring across the western limits of the desert.

It was then that Kirk noticed, almost directly above him, a thin scarf of cloud that had been a distinguishable tracery in the sky since mid-day.

He gazed up at it entranced.

It was completely motionless, catching all that outpouring of molten colour until it was first pink, then red, and finally a blood-like crimson.

Kirk was still looking up at it when his horse gave a startled neigh and shied violently.

Thinking instantly of snakes, Kirk glanced down at the trail and saw, with a shock, what it was that had frightened the animal.

It was the shapeless mass of feathers that, not so many hours before, had been a living creature that had dived through the drift of cloud to attack a trail-weary stallion.

Kirk knew then with an upsurge of excitement that no matter what difficulties he had yet to meet and overcome, the stallion was not far away. Nor for that matter was he too far distant from water. Kirk could scent it in the breeze that had suddenly sprung up, and blowing direct from the north, dispersed the thin scarf of cloud. . . .

He camped that night within a few yards of the place where Dark Fury had fought and subdued the winged demon of Sun Rock.

At midnight, a crescent moon stood high in the sky, and for the first time in many days, the breeze continued to come in strong like the remnant of a storm wind that had blown itself out on the rocky heights of a mountain range. . . .

Chapter Eleven

The fact that when leaving the scene of his encounter with the vulture, Dark Fury had followed a practically straight trail, made it possible for Kirk Merrett to set off again while it was still half light. That early start was the difference between life and death for the stallion.

Kirk rode hard for most of the day, heartened for the most part by the glimpse of mountains rising up ahead. Even when still a long way off, he could see that they were entirely different from the crumbling mass he had left behind. Apart from anything else, there was an abundance of water in those hills he was approaching. It required but half an eye to note their green appearance, even from a distance, and to see the deeper green way down on their flanks ... the green, surely, of trees growing where the ground was moist and fertile.

When at last he hit the plain of greasewood, and was able to see the hills standing out so clearly that every detail on them was revealed, he spurred his horse to greater effort, at the same time shouting to the pack animal who, since he had been running free, had been lagging behind.

It was still very hot. The heat struck upwards in shimmering waves, reflected from the sandy ground. By now, however, the endless expanse of low greasewood, here and there interspersed with yellow sagebrush, began to mark the first steep rise to the mountains. Then, at long last, Kirk was moving along the trail that led direct to the dwarf cedars growing amidst the overspill of boulders.

Soon then, he came to the deep wash with its red water ... and Dark Fury, still lying partly held in the soft, oozing sand.

Kirk drew the horses to a stumbling halt and stared down with unbelieving eyes. Could that lean, shaggy beast be the splendid stallion that had won his admiration?

A cry of compassion sprang from his lips. He hastily dismounted and crossed over to the stricken stallion. As he felt his feet sinking into the sand, he halted, wondering if the horse was not too far gone to save.

Suddenly he felt the sand sliding away a little beneath his weight. He leaped back, and as he did so, Dark Fury struggled out of the darkness that had taken from him the fear of death.

He saw, as if from a great distance, the distorted outlines of Kirk and the two horses. He had the utmost difficulty in recognising the outlines. Nothing seemed to be in focus. He was even less conscious of being a living entity. Then his heart, for so long feeble in its impulses, took on a steadier beat and life began to assert itself.

In a moment there came to him the memory of other men who had kept him captive, and it was with this memory strong in him that he saw not the young man who had once succoured him, but another who had ill-treated him and brought to his flanks the sting of the whip.

Dark Fury tried desperately to move, but the quicksand held his hindquarters, and in his weakness he was unequal to the effort necessary to get him free. His eyes rolled in the terror he experienced, showing the whites in an ominous manner; his mouth opened wide, disclosing the gleaming teeth.

Kirk backed away slowly, wondering what he could do to drag the horse out of the quicksand, at the same time asking himself if it would not be a waste of time. Dark Fury seemed so pitiable an object, and so near to dying. Would it not be better after all to shoot him and put him out of his misery?

Shocked at the thought, Kirk slipped and fell.

This seemed to rouse Dark Fury to greater terror. He uttered a piercing scream, and whilst he was still unable to struggle against the tug of the sand, he did half-raise his head, and gave Kirk a look that contained all the wild savagery of his nature. Yet, somehow, the young man felt that the savagery came from an uncontrollable fear, and that Dark Fury recognised in him his only hope of escape from an ignoble death.

Even if this was only wishful thinking on his part, Kirk knew that he could not let the stallion die without making some effort to save him.

Regaining his feet, Kirk, realising that there was only one thing he could do, hastened to get a rope.

The stallion's scream had, however, unnerved the two horses who were on a point of making off. Kirk's voice checked them before they could get into their stride, and in a matter of seconds, both were hobbled so that they could not stray far. He hurried back to Dark Fury with a coil of rope suitable for the purpose he had in mind.

Dark Fury must have sensed that purpose, and was immediately assailed with other remembrances of a similar nature. Held as he was by his hindquarters in the sand that refused to set him free, and greatly weakened by the privations he had undergone, he could only watch Kirk prepare the noose to fasten about his neck.

'Steady pal,' Kirk said quietly, hoping thus to check any tendency the stallion might have of worsening his position by struggling.

Dark Fury's head was thrust forward in his direction, the lips drawn back in a fiendish snarl.

Then the rope hissed through the air and settled cleanly over the stallion's neck.

Another scream of terror came from the animal, but was silenced immediately by the tightening of the lasso and the tugging that seemed to be heaving him out of the sand.

Kirk was pulling with all his strength, the veins on his forehead knotted with the tremendous effort he was making. It was all so unreal ... like something existing in a nightmare. Dark Fury's head thrust out towards him resembled that of some primeval creature from the swamps. The mouth was agape, the eyes again rolling with terror in their sockets.

Then the sand began to yield a little its grip on the stallion's flanks. The horse could feel his limbs sliding out of it ... then over it. His forefeet tore the firm sand with vigour.

There was a new desire in his movements now ... a desire to be free not only of the sand, but of the rope that threatened to choke him.

Kirk continued to pull with all the passion of a man demented. There was no sense of triumph in his almost superhuman efforts. He was only conscious of the need to get the stallion free of the quicksand and set him in one of the canyons amongst the hills where was fresh water and possibly lush grassland.

The endless miles he had traversed to catch up with the horse lay behind him now; the uncertainty he had endured for the last couple of days was forgotten. There was only one grim determination governing his actions now, and that was to save the stallion.

Thus he pulled and pulled, and Dark Fury himself began to thresh the sand as he essayed to regain his feet. There was, moreover, a bitter hatred in his threshing ... hatred not so much for the man who had roped him – he had already recognised the help Kirk was giving him – but hatred for the weakness that would not permit him to help himself to a greater degree.

At last he was out of the quicksand and standing on his feet. His lips were drawn back in a snarl, and as he stood before Kirk, he looked more hideous than any creature the lad had ever known.

Then his sides began to heave spasmodically as if he would vomit up much of the foul water he had drunk and which had become a slow poison in his blood. As with all horses, the effort was in vain, but he coughed up a rope of saliva.

The horse slowly recovered, and Kirk experienced a stab of fear, realising that despite his condition, the stallion could, if roused, deal him a serious injury.

There was no mistaking the change that was taking place in Dark Fury's manner. Now that he was again on his feet and on firm ground, he was full of a new surging life force that possessed sufficient vitality to take away the lean, starved look he had but a few minutes before.

Dark Fury tossed his head and gave a sharp backward tug as if to free himself of the lasso.

'Steady, boy,' Kirk said soothingly.

Dark Fury ceased to strain against the rope and stood quite still, glaring at his captor. It seemed that the effort of memory was bringing to life the time and place where he had met Kirk before. The wild, hideous look went from his eyes, and his jaws ceased to gape.

Again he tossed his head and pawed the ground restlessly.

Gently, ready for any aggressive reaction from the horse, Kirk moved back a pace or two, tightening the lasso and trying to entice the animal to follow. For a moment he felt the rope quiver as Dark Fury resisted the forward tug, then, to Kirk's unbounded delight, the stallion responded to the subtle urge to follow the pull of the rope, moving slowly, with each foot feeling the way as if he could not forget what a false step could accomplish to the unwary.

Step by step, moving with the utmost caution and never letting his eyes leave those of the stallion, Kirk succeeded in leading the animal farther and farther away from the wash of red water and the dreaded quicksand. His own two horses stood away off watching. As if bound by a common fear, they moved closer together as the stallion was brought towards them, each animal standing taut until Dark Fury, still obeying the tug of the lasso, was led in the direction of the cedars.

'Steady, boy,' Kirk said, over and over again, whenever Dark Fury attempted to pull against him.

After a few minutes, Kirk paused, and regarded the stallion with misgiving. He was feeling none too sure about him. He felt that the horse was following him all too easily, as if he had no spirit left in him.

Kirk then recalled the very first time he set eyes on the stallion in that hastily erected corral on Burke's showground. How different then had been Dark Fury's appearance! The young man remembered too how he had wished that the stallion belonged to him so that they could journey the great plains together, not just as man and horse, but as companions.

There was a thrill in his blood as he stared at Dark Fury standing so quietly at the end of the rope. The horse surely belonged to none but him now. His wish had come true, and in such an unexpected manner.

The lasso ran slack as he stood remembering and thinking. At the back of his mind was a strange, recurring impulse ... to let the stallion go and merely content himself with following him to that northland range he was so clearly bent on reaching.

As he thought thus, his fingers began to nervously pay out the rope so that it slackened still more letting the noose run free about Dark Fury's neck.

He thought chaotically: 'Mebbe he'll not go far ... knowin' I've saved him. ... Mebbe in the end he'll come to me of his own free will. ...'

Kirk was jerked out of his dreaming just as he remembered the fabled Lost Canyon. Swiftly, and without the slightest warning, Dark Fury had lowered his head and slipped free of the rope. The muscles rippled under the skin of his shoulders. More than ever was he becoming the horse Kirk had admired in the corral of the showground, with a return of his old indomitable spirit.

Dark Fury did no more than toss his head arrogantly, and without the slightest sign of haste started to move off towards the mountains and a pass that was clearly visible less than half a mile away.

Kirk let him go, noticing that in spite of the improvement in his appearance during the last few minutes, his pace was slow and laboured. It was clear that although he had certainly recovered from his terrifying experiences in the quicksand, he was still very weak.

Nevertheless, some thirty minutes later Dark Fury had succeeded in climbing up to the break in the mountain wall, and pausing only for a second or two, entered on to the divide and disappeared from view.

The young man who had watched his progress sensed that beyond the divide was the grassland and water the stallion needed to recover his full vigour, and realising that his own two animals were also in need of water and rest, he hurriedly returned to them and was soon *en route* to that new country that lay beyond the pass. ...

The cedars growing amongst the overspill of rocks were deeply rooted, and appeared sturdy in comparison to those cedars Kirk had seen in the vicinity of Sun Rock.

Kirk climbed slowly, leading his two horses over a trail that, like those other trails he had traversed across the desert, held in places the impress of Dark Fury's hooves. At first the slope was sandy, then as the trees became scattered, so did the ascent change in character. The last of the sagebrush vanished, and directly ahead lay a slope of black rock, polished by the many centuries of wind and rain it had known, and broken in places so that it contained long grooves that, in times of rain, were watershoots.

Kirk's feet slipped on the rock, and he had difficulty in maintaining his balance. The horses, however, seemed more surefooted, and after half a mile of steady climbing, he came close to the almost perpendicular wall of mountain that kept the divide over which Dark Fury had gone.

As he progressed alongside the cliff, he glimpsed water a-plenty, glimmering in deeply recessed grooves. Close to the break in the mountain, he saw trees growing grotesquely out of the living rock, trees, gnarled and distorted, some shrunken and grey, others green and flourishing, but all of them old ... very old.

Breathless, Kirk was forced to make a short halt, while his horses stood nervously pawing the ground.

After an encouraging remark to the leading animal, he resumed the ascent, moving cautiously as he came to a point where the cliff began to fall steeply towards the divide.

Because of his two horses, both heavily laden, after hitting the rock trail he had deviated a little to the east, and whilst at the earlier stages of the climb the ascent had been easy enough, here it was not so. The trail was less secure and went straight up against the mountain wall until it ran beneath an overhang, and was little more than a tunnel, smooth as marble.

Then the cliff fell back and the trail came out on to a wide grassy ledge. A moment later, Kirk looked over the divide.

95

It was an entirely new world he saw.

The pass slipped steeply away to a canyon thrusting northwards into the very heart of the mountain range. There was no gloom anywhere despite the height of the uprising walls that supported the pinnacles high above. A fall of water was the most outstanding spectacle that first attracted Kirk's attention until he saw, midway down the canyon, an enormous arch of varicoloured rock, and beneath it, grazing on the greenest of green grass, Dark Fury.

Kirk thought impulsively: 'Is this Lost Canyon?'

The impatient movement of the two horses behind him broke the significance of the thought, and giving a tug at the halter of the leading animal, he started the descent into the valley.

He was perhaps half-way down the slope when the clear light began to go, not slowly as would have happened out on the desert, but quickly. Kirk hastened on, wishing to camp the night on the floor of the canyon where he could set his horses at liberty to graze as Dark Fury was grazing on what was rich grassland.

Fortunately the descent became easier as the floor of the canyon came nearer, and while behind him, the pass was darkening with night, there was still sufficient light remaining in the canyon to enable him to finally reach the grassland.

He was not a moment too soon, for he had scarcely taken the packs from the horses when the entire valley filled with gloom, and within a matter of seconds, the only remaining object visible was the varicoloured arch.

The most satisfactory camp he had yet made was set up under a clump of silver spruce which grew close against the southern wall of the mountain.

Within an hour of his reaching the valley, Kirk was resting comfortably, wrapped in a blanket, since it grew cold as the night hours wore on. The flickering glow of his campfire threw the shadows of the spruces in gesticulating outlines against the cliff until they resembled dancers. In moments, they seemed to be reaching up and up as if towards the new moon that rose athwart the mountain's rim and brought a silver radiance to the arch and to the spout of water which, in the quietness, had assumed the voice of a many-piped organ, playing a sonorous fugue until Kirk fell asleep and the sound was no more than a faint echo in his ears. . . .

The white stars and sickle moon, moving across the fabric of the night sky, patterned the passing hours.

Chapter Twelve

The canyon was situated in the group of mountains that, in the west, terminated in the Raft River Range. The entire group formed a barrier between the desert lands of Utah and the more fertile country of Idaho. Towering high into the blue sky at sunrise on that first morning when Kirk and Dark Fury took refuge in the canyon, were the jagged peaks of the main ridge which rose in fluted columns from the level floor of the valley. There were deep indentations in some of the cliffs which appeared to resemble smaller canyons verdant with cedar and spruce.

Daybreak in the canyon had been a slow gathering of light that seemed to spill over the eastern cliffs like a torrent of crystal-clear water. Then as the sun itself sent long fingers tracing colours across the sky, many rainbow hues appeared where the fall of water poured from a crevasse more than five hundred feet up. The lake it formed was blue like the sky above it, and it was a mirror that reflected the shapes of the uprising cliffs and the sun-sparkle of the water-spout. North-west of the lake was a firmly set trail leading to the head of the canyon where it twisted up to a divide similar to the one that Dark Fury and Kirk had come over the previous evening.

Whilst the clear light of day revealed the charm of the canyon which evening had managed to conceal, it also served to bring out the almost delicate tracery of the magnificent bridge that completely spanned the vast amphitheatre from east to west.

The arch, of natural formation, similar to many such spectacles in canyons ranging all along the Wyoming–Colorado border, was etched in a perfect half-circle, and Kirk, busying himself with replenishing his camp fire prior to preparing his breakfast, could not help pausing in his efforts to gaze for long minutes at a stretch at the span. There was something about it that moved him to a strange emotion, and he could only regain his composure by concentrating his attention on his two horses who were feeding peaceably on grass that was smooth like that of cultivated turf.

His next surprise sprang out of the perfection of that grassland until he realised that its very smoothness came from an abundance of rabbits that also fed on it.

Then as his gaze wandered down the entire length of the valley, he saw, within the region of the arch, that Dark Fury was also busy grazing. The stallion seemed to be recovering from his terrifying experiences in the desert.

Seeing how contented Dark Fury was at his grazing, Kirk had the feeling that he was likely to remain in the canyon for many days. The young fellow immediately came to the decision to set up a more permanent camp, and then looked around for places suitable for the setting of snares for rabbits.

That first day in the canyon was perhaps one of the happiest he had ever spent in his life. Next day he knew without any uncertainty that he was not mistaken about the prolonged stay he was to make in the canyon. Dark Fury showed not the slightest inclination to leave.

Indeed, the stallion was only too ready to remain in a place where grazing was so good and where there was an abundance of fresh water. The sickness of his body was fast being replaced by a new strength, and after a while he found another way to refresh himself. Acting as if by instinct, he stood for long periods in the lake, staring at the fall of water and gradually moving up closer and closer to it. It seemed to attract him, and finally, after testing the depth of the water and the rock basin into which the falls emptied with a roar, he began to approach even closer until he was standing with his body drenched in the spray. Then he started to investigate the twisting ropes of water, and for almost an hour stood under a shelving ledge of rock while the spume went tossing and boiling over him in an arc no less splendid than the bridge that spanned the canyon.

Although Kirk had no idea what attracted Dark Fury to the falls, the stallion himself possessed vague memories of another such torrent cascading down a rather steeper mountain height in another canyon vaster than this one on the borderlands of Idaho.

With the return of his strength, certain other nerve cells revived, and with their rebirth came a stronger singing in his bloodstream, until be began to remember much more clearly those other things that had been intimately associated with his life in the Valley of Lost Rivers.

The spume of water was one of the memories that seemed more vivid than some of the others, so that the very shape of the fall assumed the character of that other fall he knew in a far distant canyon. Thus for long spells at a time he stood close to the tossing spray remembering, and placing firmly in his mind's eye every contour of the hills on that home range, while yet knowing that the trail to that northland country was long and tortuous.

In every way, Dark Fury was becoming more than ever possessed of a knowledge that had been the knowledge of his wild ancestors. As in the desert his widely flaring nostrils had told him the way he should go to reach water, so now did he begin to know the exact direction he must take if he would return to the place where he had once lived in freedom; and the trail lay along the twisting track that climbed up out of the canyon to disappear over that northern divide.

The knowledge was more than just mere orientation. It was like an extended vision that saw far beyond the boundaries of mountains and valleys, and glimpsed away off the place he knew as his own special range, distinct from all other ranges because he had been born close to it, and had roamed it since his colt-hood days.

The time for his departure, however, was not yet near. He had first to recuperate and build up sufficient reserves of strength to carry him over the many long miles he must travel before even approaching the outposts of the Valley of the Lost Rivers.

Dark Fury was rapidly assuming a wisdom that had been the

wisdom of his sire who, in the long years that had gone, had been one of the great horses of the west.

That afternoon as he stood in the rock basin with the cool swirl of the water about his legs and the toss of the spray over his back, he sensed, creeping over him, a contentment such as he had only known in the days before his great adversity when man had come and taken him by surprise. In fact, so contented was he that he remained for a very long time contemplating the fall and turned broadside to the penetrating rays of the westering sun so that he could enjoy their warmth without leaving the spot that reminded him so much of his own Lost Canyon way off beyond the far horizon of mountain peaks.

Early next morning when grazing under the shadow of the arch, Dark Fury heard Kirk's horses uttering joyful cries. He raised his head the better to watch them. They were both running after Kirk who had the appearance of trying to hide from them in play.

The stallion was much intrigued.

To and fro went the horses, following the leaping shape of the young man. At last Kirk stopped and the excited animals went cantering up to him, both with tossing heads and prancing feet. He then proceeded to feed them with tufts of grass he had gathered in his leaping.

Dark Fury, stirred by an increasing sense of curiosity, moved in their direction. His steps were cautious. Even so, he made no attempt to conceal his interest. His eyes were shining brightly and his ears were pricked as if he sought to catch every faint sound.

He was less than thirty yards distant before he stopped. Kirk, aware of his approach, was watching him with undisguised excitement. He felt that maybe after all the stallion was going to accept him in much the same manner as the other animals had done. When, however, Dark Fury came to a halt, clearly hesitant to proceed further, Kirk did not experience any great dismay. That, he felt, was to be expected.

The stallion obviously was not going all out to accept man as a friend without first being satisfied that there was not likely to be a repetition of his earlier experiences. In time, maybe, he would learn that his trust would not again be betrayed. Perhaps then he would resign himself to being a man's horse. . . . Maybe then the way to Lost Canyon would be readily opened, the stallion leading him to the place of his own free will.

Kirk no sooner found himself thinking about the Lost Canyon when Dark Fury started to back slowly away. Suddenly, and for the good reason that he could not restrain himself, he turned about and went racing across the valley, his tail flying out behind him. There was joy in his leaping when he came to a small stream which he took in one upward bound.

Watching Dark Fury showing off his paces in such a startling manner, Kirk knew that the horse was well on the way to being his old self once again, and put the rapid recovery down to the rich grazing of the valley.

He was unable to guess the enormous vitality the stallion possessed and his exceptional powers of recuperation. Near as he had been to death when Kirk discovered him in the wash, once free of the quicksand and up on his feet, the old fierce will that had sustained him through many trials had asserted itself anew.

The next few days passed without undue incident, Dark Fury keeping close to the waterfall and Kirk remaining in that part of the canyon where he could hunt at will.

Then one evening the young man discovered the lair of a bobcat. The creature had kittens too, and was likely to prove a formidable opponent if suddenly cornered. He was about to return to his camp when Kirk glimpsed the creature coming down off the nearby slope carrying a hare.

The cat saw him and stood with arched back.

If it had not been for the fact she had kittens to rear, Kirk would have shot her. As it was, he decided to leave her unmolested, and made a slow retreat, keeping the cat within sight until he was at a distance when he could turn his back without fear of attack.

Meanwhile, Kirk confined his hunting activities well away from the lair, and hoped against hope to attract Dark Fury to him as on that other occasion.

He had been a week in the canyon when the next unexpected

meeting with the bobcat took place. He had been up investigating the head of the canyon, taking only the saddle horse and leaving the other grazing close to the camp. His hope to reach the northern divide and survey the country beyond was frustrated by the strange manoeuvres of Dark Fury.

Kirk began to ride back to the camp as quickly as he could.

He saw the valley from an entirely different angle as he came hastening down the mountain trail, but his impressions were vague because he was much concerned at the antics of Dark Fury and the horse he had left in the region of the camp.

The stallion was snaking up and down the pasture some fifty yards from the camp site, while the erstwhile pack horse gave him the impression of being petrified with fear.

Then Kirk understood.

The animal was not afraid of Dark Fury, but of something else. Close to the tent and lying beside the cache he had made was the bobcat.

It took Kirk the best part of fifteen minutes to reach the neighbourhood of the arch, but the moment he came galloping under it, Dark Fury, who had succeeded in getting himself into a position that gave him the advantage over the enemy, heard the sound of his rapid approach. So too did the bobcat who instantly jumped to her feet and made off with a rabbit gripped between her teeth.

The creature had scarcely got into her stride when Dark Fury went racing after her.

Kirk reined in his horse and sat tensely in the saddle, watching.

The cat was quick and lithe in her movements, but she was being overtaken in a manner that threatened her with destruction before she could reach the security of her lair.

Without warning, she suddenly turned, and with arched back, faced the oncoming stallion. When it seemed that Dark Fury would be unable to break the spurt of speed he was making towards her, he swung a little to the right, and, as Kirk calculated it, he did so not a moment too soon.

The bobcat had leaped!

Even as Dark Fury swung around, the cat retrieved what, for her, had been a precarious situation. Her ruse had broken the stallion's turn of speed, and she took advantage of the respite. Picking up the rabbit again, she was off once more, this time running a straight line to the lair under the slope of the southern cliff.

By the time Dark Fury had recovered from her surprise tactics, the cat had reached the boulder-strewn slope, and vanished into the lair.

When Kirk started to ride into the camp, Dark Fury trotted off in a half-circle and was soon back in his favourite place, grazing quietly as if the event with the bobcat had not taken place. The young man, however, found that the pack horse was nervous, constantly glancing towards the cliff where the cat's lair was situated.

On examination, Kirk discovered that the cache had been thoroughly destroyed by the cat. Very little was left in it, and the bones and bits of fur scattered round about told of her feasting.

He felt none too happy to know that the creature possessed sufficient courage to invade his camp. Before he could quite make up his mind how best to circumvent any further visit the cat might contemplate, the creature herself took the next decisive step. She quit the lair under cover of darkness, taking her kittens with her.

She then began the trek to the new lair she had in mind to occupy, a place far up the slope and hidden in a crevasse difficult for anything but a bird to reach unless possessed, as she and her kittens were, of a sure-footed way of negotiating the narrow ledges that slanted upwards at terrifying angles.

Her move, however, proved to be quite unnecessary, for early next morning as a mocking bird called out across the valley, Dark Fury, conscious of a great unrest, moved up towards the northern trail. By sun-up, he was climbing steadily towards the divide.

He was feeling lusty and strong once again, and, as if he knew that the terrors of the desert lay far behind him and that ahead was more familiar country, he pressed on with assurance and a light heart.

Kirk awakened late that morning, and was surprised to find the stallion nowhere visible under the arch, nor yet in the valley itself.

He then surveyed the surrounding hills and glimpsed Dark Fury high up on that northern divide ... a motionless figure etched against the blue of the sky.

Kirk knew then that another stage in the great trek to the fabled Lost Canyon had begun.

An hour later, he had broken camp and was hard on the stallion's trail. The last sound he heard as he topped the rise was the repeated calling of the mocking bird. Nothing else could he hear. Even the roar of the waterfall was lost in the distance he had covered.

Just before he reached the divide, he felt compelled to rein in his horses and glance back.

The walls of the canyon sloped away at a dizzy angle to end in the loose scree which, in turn, gave way to the verdant stretch of grassland. Kirk noticed not so much the pasture or the rich colouring of the valley as he did the iris-hued arch ... a splendid semi-circle spanning the valley from east to west and which, at some remote period of its history, had been no more than molten rock gushing out from some hidden lava-hole. The million, million years or more that had dawned and gone, had solidified it, and brought about so great a change that life could now dwell in the valley and graze in contentment on the lush pasture that time had brought into being.

Then, as had been his experience in that other canyon on Sun Rock, Kirk felt a little of the agelessness of the world, a little too, of its majesty and beauty.

As he jerked his horses into movement, he did so after the manner of one who was an intruder in the world ... a mere whisper in the wind. Indeed, a man of no account.

The sound of the mocking bird died away in his ears, and as he came out on to the divide, he could hear it no longer. The very next moment, all his thoughts had gone filtering away on the rush of the air streams that came beating up against him.

He gasped with amazement.

The new world was an even vaster world, and in it were many new things to be seen and conquered.

For a while, he sat taut in the saddle, gazing down upon it, and all the while the timeless wind sang its ancient song and told him of the great distances it had covered and of the many mysteries, more stupendous than the canyon behind him, that it had traversed in as little as a day's march.

There was joy then in Kirk's heart, and a great sense of well-being. He rode down into that new world like a conqueror!

Book Three
Forlorn River Valley

Chapter Thirteen

Dark Fury's crossing of that northern divide leading direct to the State border mountain range did not go unnoticed. Nor for that matter did Kirk's journey towards Idaho pass without special note being made of the occasion.

High up on one of the ridges opposite the divide, from which could be seen not only the trail into Utah, but also, northward, the entire fall of the country towards the distant Snake River Plain in Idaho, was a solitary horseman. Motionless, yet with eyes as keen as those of any eagle whose name he bore, was an Indian of the Cœur D'Alenes. Even the brown and white mustang on which he sat so well was as still as its rider.

For some days now, the Indian had ridden up to the ridge, setting out from his camp soon after dawn. Washakie, his leader, gifted as he was with his special knowledge of the ways of the wild, had guessed accurately the route Dark Fury was likely to take in his efforts to reach the nearest fertile plains to the great Utah desert. Indeed, Washakie had even reckoned on the stallion crossing this very divide. Not that this was very difficult to guess, for the divide, leading up out of the Blue Creek Hills was, after all, the only possible trail. Moreover, it was one that had been in constant use for centuries, not only by migratory animals, but also by the few itinerant travellers who roamed from Stateline to Stateline.

Once over the divide, Dark Fury stood gazing down the sharp descent to the valley below. The trail was clearly marked. It went winding down to a stretch of scrubland and sagebrush, only to rise again to the scarred slopes of the hills that supported the east to west trail from Snowville to Kelton Pass. Westward of the pass rose the snow-clad peaks of the Raft River Range itself.

The stallion tested the atmosphere. There was confidence in his action. Even so, there was a great restlessness in him. The sight of the endless hills ahead brought to his senses a recurring familiarity that gave a surer beat to his heart and a swifter surging of the blood through his veins. His ears were erect, his muzzle thrust out as he sought to sift every clue he got from the fast-veering wind.

At last he gave a short backward glance at the divide, and glimpsed only the irregular shape of the highest peak on the far side of the canyon. Nothing else could he see. He shook himself and started the steep descent. His progress was marked with care. The trail was broken and pitted with small chasms in which an unwary animal could so easily break a leg and bring complete disaster upon himself.

Dark Fury was about halfway down when he suddenly stopped. He was inclined to suspicion and his eyes searched intently the scrubland below. There was a movement among it that held his attention. As he watched, his nostrils again hard at work testing the air, something in his bloodstream warned the stallion to act with the utmost caution.

For some minutes Dark Fury was as motionless as the Indian on the opposing ridge. He also was intent on watching the progress of four riders across the brushland.

The Indian was quicker than the stallion in determining who the riders were. He recognised them the moment they broke cover and rode out into the open.

Like Washakie, the four riders had guessed the divide the stallion was likely to cross to reach Snake River Plain. The men were Luke Unwin and his companions. Instead of travelling east across the great Salt Lake Desert, they had gone northwards, keeping to the mountains and finally following the river trail until within sight of the Raft River group. By so doing, they had avoided the long and weary journey across the desert, and in a measure had shortened their trek by many days. Moreover, they were sure of the trail Dark Fury was likely to take when once out of the desert. It was the very trail along which they had brought him after taking him from his ranging territory in the valley of Little Lost River.

Rigid, the Indian continued to watch both the advancing figures below in the valley and also the stallion who stood high up on the mountain trail. One other he saw too – Kirk, coming up over the divide with his two animals.

Suddenly he knew that the stallion had recognised the riders down on the scrubland, for he had thrown up his head and was displaying all the anger he so clearly felt.

The Indian vanished abruptly from his position on the ridge. He started off northward to summon help from those others of his tribe who were also watching for Dark Fury at scattered outposts along the northern trail.

Meanwhile, Luke Unwin and his companions, riding slowly and on the alert, had seen the stallion high up on that mountain trail. Like the Indian, they also saw Kirk coming up through the divide.

Unwin was wildly delighted. He gesticulated as he headed the others along the sagebrush trail. The hours spent waiting for just this very moment had been well worthwhile.

'Look!' he shouted to Maitland who was riding close behind him. 'Dark Fury . . . he's on the way down. . . . We'll have him soon enough now. . . .'

As he reined in his horse, bringing the others to a stumbling halt, he pointed to the sagebrush that grew all along the foothills, and edged the very trail Dark Fury was on.

'We'll force the hoss to turn off into that small canyon there. . . .' He indicated a break in the mountain that was more of a deep cleft than the canyon Unwin fondly imagined it to be. 'Fire the scrub an' the crittur 'll have to turn off from the trail.' He laughed. 'One thing's certain sure. He won't be makin' it back up the trail because of the young feller up there on the divide. . . .'

'Burke's feller, you mean,' Tim Corson broke in.

Unwin shaded his eyes with one hand and stared upwards.

'Aye ... could be him. Still the hoss ain't likely to risk goin' back. We can rope him if we drive him into the canyon. ...'

'What's wrong with lettin' him come down off the trail? We could round him up easily enough here.' Corson spoke slowly.

Enos Wills and Bill Maitland were inclined to agree.

Luke scoffed at them for being fools.

'Round him up easy enough, you say?' he remarked to Corson. He shook his head. 'That one's too canny a crittur to get caught a second time unless it's done on the quiet. We sure couldn't take him by surprise in this valley. Why, he'd run like the black devil he is, an' we'd never catch him. Nope! The canyon idea is best.'

'Mebbe, you're right, boss,' Maitland admitted.

'Ain't I alwis bin right?'

'Mebbe.'

'Whatja mean ... mebbe?'

Unwin sensed that Maitland was disputing his judgement on certain matters relating to the past, recalling how easily the stallion had been taken from him by the Indians.

'I ain't disputin' you're right most times, boss,' Maitland said soothingly. 'I think mebbe you've gotta good idea here anyways.'

Temporarily mollified, Luke gave instructions for firing the scrub.

Three-quarters of an hour later, Dark Fury, still well up on the trail, saw the leaping bursts of flame, and the drift of smoke across the lower foothills.

He snorted with fear, knowing the points of light to be his most dreaded enemy ... fire! The dry grass, the first to be kindled, spluttered and blazed furiously, the smoke increasing as the leaping flames caught the scrub and completely segregated the trail from the valley enclosed between the two groups of mountains.

Kirk Merrett had not long since crossed the divide, and seeing Dark Fury way down on the trail, felt that he could now more easily keep him in sight. He decided to change mounts, and in a matter of seconds had transferred the saddle from one animal to the other.

He was about to mount the newly saddled horse when he saw the white bursts of smoke sweeping up from below. Focusing his eyes on the stallion he saw him rear from the trail, taking what, from a distance, appeared to be a ledge that wound eastwards along the shoulder of the mountain.

Immediately then, because the fire in the valley was spreading rapidly, Kirk was rewarded with the sight of the four riders who, till that moment, had been hidden from his view. He noticed, with dismay, that two of them were riding along the scrubland, setting burning brands amongst the brushwood so that within a matter of minutes, the entire foot of the slope was edged with fire.

Kirk needed no further intimation to know what was really taking place. The four cowpunchers from the circus had, at last, caught up with the stallion, and were intent on driving him to some precarious place where he would the more easily fall victim to their ropes.

Dark Fury, however, was already traversing the ledge as if to escape from the flames which were creeping up towards the trail. He had recovered from his fear at the sight of those whom he hated, and his progress along the ledge was slow and indicative of the caution he exercised. There was no sign of panic in his movements.

The smoke was now rolling up the hillside in white whorls, hiding for long minutes at a time the leaping, crackling flames.

Kirk, anxious to keep the stallion in sight, mounted the horse which was growing nervous. The other animal, now laden with the packs, seemed less highly strung and was waiting almost patiently for his master to press on down the track.

Conscious of the hazards of the downward twist of the trail, Kirk was compelled to hold his mount well in hand, for he was none too sure of foot and shied at every boulder he encountered.

Then quite unexpectedly disaster overtook him. Despite the caution, the now terrified animal caught his right foot in one of the chasms which earlier, Dark Fury had avoided with such ease. He gave a piercing scream of terror as he stumbled, throwing Kirk.

The pack horse in panic raced back in the direction of the now distant divide. And, as Kirk struggled desperately to check his rolling, scream after scream came from the fallen animal now making a valiant effort to regain his feet.

At last Kirk succeeded in breaking his impetus downhill. Bruised and shaken, he made his way back to the spot where the horse continued to thresh the ground in agony and despair.

The very instant he reached the animal, Kirk saw with dismay what had happened; his leg was broken.

His reaction was instantaneous. Once before he had been faced with the same decision – the decision that all men who love horses must make and act upon. His hand flew to his holster, and having satisfied himself that the other animal was too far up the track to witness what was taking place, he drew his revolver, and releasing the safety catch, prepared to pull the trigger.

For a split second, the stricken beast ceased his agonised threshing, his eyes turned to Kirk in supplication.

'It's the only way old timer!' Kirk muttered, on an intake of breath, and the next moment there was a resounding echo as he fired. As Kirk rose from the kneeling posture he had adopted to ensure making no mistake in his aim, it seemed that the creature's eyes were still instinct with life. It was an illusion, of course, but none the less, Kirk felt a queer feeling pass through him. Then to his surprise, the lids dropped slowly over those staring eyes, and the jaws lolled open.

The curious illusion that had disturbed him was gone. As he looked down at the body, the animal was just another creature betrayed by the trail it had so recently trodden. Yet, Kirk sensed that somewhere out on the mountain, the Spirit of Fur and Hide was awaiting the errant animal to guide him to the great grazing fields of eternity.

Sighing with the strange burden of his thoughts, he stroked the lifeless head. Then lifting the saddle from the still warm body, and without a further glance at the carcass, he made his way up the trail to recapture the other horse.

By this time, one continuous line of fire flickered along the foot of the mountain, but contrary to Unwin's expectations, did not penetrate far up the trail owing to the scarcity of grass on the upper reaches.

Moreover, the ledge Dark Fury followed led to a point well above the canyon Unwin had visualised. What was even more important, the ledge itself thrust upwards to broaden into a rock plateau that, less than two miles distant, at the head of the valley, joined the east to west trail from Snowville to Kelton Pass.

The stallion made slow progress along the ledge. Each step had to be chosen with care, each turn made so as to avoid slipping on the flaking rock. Nevertheless, in little over thirty minutes, he had covered more than half a mile, and had negotiated the more treacherous places by keeping close to the shelving cliffs that soared in bold, straight lines to the main ridge high above. In spite of the care he exercised, his movements were full of determination, and the only pauses he made were when he felt compelled to gaze down at the valley below to ascertain if the four men he feared had attempted to pursue him.

Good fortune, however, was with him that day. The fire Unwin had so quickly brought into being with a view to trapping the stallion, had proved his own undoing.

As so often happened between two opposing groups of mountains, the wind, shaped by the predominant peaks, seldom travelled a straight course. On this particular day, coming as it did direct from the north, it blew from off Black Pine Peak way out in Idaho, and meeting the ridge of hills adjacent to Kelton Pass, veered west to find itself confined within the horse-shoe formation of the Raft River Mountains. Strengthened here with the varying cross-currents from the west, it became a steady blast that went sweeping back along the ridge to finally engulf the valley which Unwin had fired.

The valley, for all the fertility of the canyons it contained, was quite dry, and in no time, the spear-points of fire which Unwin had hoped to confine to the foothills, encroached on the main part of the valley. Fanned by the ever-rising wind currents, it went leaping from bush to bush, and soon was menacing the entire depression from east to west.

The cowpunchers were not long in discovering how badly their plan had miscarried. They were also completely cut off from the trail which Dark Fury had been following when first they glimpsed him. The only course open was to ride westward, leaving the stallion to pursue his solitary trek to safety many miles to the east.

This was not quite so easily accomplished as at first seemed possible. The riders were widely scattered, and Unwin, shouting loudly that they must leave the valley, became aware of an exceptionally strong current of air funnelling down through a gap a little below Kelton Pass. This broadly distributed airstream caused the fire to rise with greater intensity, and the flames swept in a crackling rustle across the whole width of the depression.

Unwin continued to shout to his companions who had already swung about to essay a speedy escape. Unfortunately for them, the floor of the valley sloped to a centre thickly overgrown with dead greasewood. It required but a few flying cinders to set it ablaze, and from then onwards, it was a race against time. The fire took on a new lease of life, and fanned by the wind, sped more rapidly than ever.

The four horsemen raced like fury before it, each man a gesticulating, shouting automaton, no longer guiding their horses but leaving it entirely to the beasts to put as much distance as was possible between themselves and the dreaded flames. Indeed, the horses moved with thundering hooves and tossing manes, terrified out of their lives and only anxious to escape from the inferno behind them. They were no longer conscious of their riders save when a voice shrieked at them or a booted spur stung their flanks: and all the while the wind was coming in steadily against them, only to encounter the hot air currents from the fire and billow back, heavy with smoke and heat. . . .

In every way, Unwin's gang was literally running a gauntlet of flame, and continued so to run until all four men were well clear of the blazing valley, and were within ranging distance of the foothills of the Raft River group, many miles to the west.

Until late in the afternoon, the flames continued to grow and flare across the valley. Where the ground was blackened and the scrubland destroyed, whorls of smoke went drifting along the flanks of the hills, and it was only towards nightfall that the full extent of the fire became visible, for then, in the half shadows, the whole floor of the valley glowed, and was alive with flickers of light.

Not next day, nor for many a day to come, would Luke Unwin and his gang ride up the valley to menace the stallion in the region of Kelton Pass.

The way to Snake River Plain and the wild country beyond was open!

Chapter Fourteen

Across the entire valley, very low down in the west, the fire flickered all the long night through. No sound of it, however, reached up the mountain slopes. There, the quietness of the night was the quietness of hills grown hoary with age. No movement either was there on that lonely pass trail where earlier, a stallion had moved, and a young man, with a sense of regret in his heart, had followed, leading a frightened horse alongside something that lay stark in a silence greater than even that of the mountains.

Soon, only bleached bones would lie on the trail where man so seldom trod, and only an occasional night bird wandered and called. . . .

Nothing more!

The death of a horse on a lonely pass trail was little more than an incident in the eternity of time the mountains had known. What mattered was the present and that which was to be the future . . . the brightness of the sun at noonday or the silver glow of the moon when night stood triumphant on the hill-tops. The past was of small importance in the great world of the wild!

Kirk Merrett certainly had no thought of anything save the future when, following along the ledge Dark Fury had taken some hours before, he came at last to the final upward sweep that opened out on to the rock plateau not a great distance from the east-to west trail.

In that time, he had witnessed the hurried retreat of Luke Unwin and his gang from the valley, and saw how the encroaching flames had harried them so that they rode faster than any horsemen had ridden before. That their exit from the scene, temporary though it might be, had been so easily accomplished, brought a glow of satisfaction to the young man's heart. Dark Fury had certainly been close to disaster when he set off down the trail, and it was the gang's own efforts to scare him that had eventually proved his salvation.

That, in itself, was something to hearten one for the future.

Then at last he came out on to the trail that followed the main ridge of the mountains bordering the plains of Idaho. No sight of vast horizons had ever thrilled him more than the glimpse he had of Idaho from such a high elevation.

It was night to evening when he came at last to Kelton Pass, and through the divide gazed down upon the Raft River country, the winding streak of the river itself seeming like a silver ribbon rolling on and on into the infinitude of silence and distance. The mountains on either side thrust ragged shoulders towards the great Snake River Plain more than two hundred miles to the north, with Black Pine Peak scarcely more than twenty-five miles away.

Kirk, reining his horse, contemplated the vastness of the new country which he guessed was Dark Fury's country.

The sunset hour was bringing untold colour and beauty to the hills. Each peak stood clearly revealed, the mid-distant sageland glowing red and purple, while at one point, the Raft River spilled like molten gold over falls that caught the sunset glow.

As Kirk continued to gaze entranced, feeling that somewhere on the sageland, the stallion was possibly searching for a place to bed down for the night, the cliffs of Black Pine Peak changed from orange to a deep red and from red back to orange again as the westering sun swung down behind Cache Peak that lay far to the west. Softly then, came night to the hills and plains, with a slow dying of colour on the sageland and a hesitant fading away of the river and falls. . . .

Kirk pitched his camp beside a protective cliff on the pass, hearing faintly, as he did so, the far-off challenging cry of some creature who feared none and was prepared to fight with his life for the freedom he had so recently gained.

With a surge of elation, Kirk recognised the cry as coming from Dark Fury, and nodded his head with satisfaction. Despite the hazards of the day, he was still within reasonable distance of the horse.

As he prepared his supper, way down on the plain, Dark Fury rested within the security of some aspens that stood like sentinels where the tents of night were pitched in rising mist. . . .

On the other side of the range, the valley continued to smoulder and glow, whereas on the stallion's side of the hills it was very peaceful indeed. Once or twice a coyote howled to the moon, and a night bird gave reply. But for these sounds, there was nothing to disturb the stallion who, having eaten his fill on grassland that was cold and fresh to his tongue, slept standing beneath the aspen whose branches covered him and gave him full protection from the chilly winds that came blowing from off Black Pine Peak.

Night seemed of short duration, for no sooner had Dark Fury dozed than the mighty kindling of the dawn began behind the hills of the east, and soon the whole skyline was a blazing gold. . . .

Such a gold it was too, that morning . . . strident like a bugle blast against the blue. There was hardly a cloud to be seen, and certainly no wind.

When Dark Fury awoke and moved from under the shelter of the aspen, he turned his head and looked about him. The entire scene lay green and remote in the early morning light. The sageland stretched away in purple and grey, while away off, the river flowed gleaming towards the far horizon of mountains that rose tier upon tier to join the sprawling Bannock Range that thrust northwards to the great unwinding of the Snake River.

The stallion was easy in mind, and when he discerned a pool not a great distance off, he walked slowly towards it, cropping the grass as he went. He was not conscious of any urgent need to be on his way. Now that the night was gone, and with it, all sign of those who were his enemies, he was relaxed, his canyon sanctuary would be reached soon enough. He knew the trail he must follow.

All at once he raised his head. Men were riding up across the sageland; they were approaching in his direction. Snorting with annoyance, the stallion stood quite still watching them. Despite his growing suspicion, he knew instinctively that they were not the men who had fired the valley the previous evening. Neither were they riding with any display of haste.

Nevertheless, Dark Fury leaped away from the trail he had been following, poised to run and hesitating only long enough to test the air currents. He then began to gallop towards the first of the foothills that rose directly in the north and around the foot of which he could see the gleam of a river.

The horsemen merely halted, watching the stallion depart. They were obviously not out to trail him across the plain.

One then pointed up to the divide. Coming down off the mountain was Kirk Merrett, leading his horse to avoid a repetition of the disaster of the previous day.

The horsemen, all Cœur D'Alenes, started to ride in the direction of the mountain slopes, completely ignoring the stallion who, by now, was running without effort to the hill and the river that flowed around it.

Kirk was met by the Indians the instant he came off the mountain trail.

The leader greeted him gravely.

'Welcome to wild hoss country,' he said.

Kirk did not know how to answer. He had recognised the Indians, immediately, and knew that he had nothing to fear from them. He had, however, been greatly surprised to witness their indifference towards Dark Fury. He had fully expected to see them make some attempt to round him up.

'You no longer interested in the black hoss?' he asked at last.

The Indian smiled. His companions merely looked on with expressionless faces.

'Him safe in his own country,' the leader replied to Kirk's question. 'In two mebbe three moons, him be in Lost Canyon, way over beyond the land of the Twin Buttes. . . .'

Kirk strove to hide his interest but the Indian's next words showed that he had not altogether succeeded.

'Lost Canyon known only to wild hoss. You no follow him there.'

Kirk shrugged his shoulders.

'You don't want me to follow him further?'

The Indian smiled again.

'We no message for you. Washakie himself keep word he gave you. You follow stallion as you please. We seek to stop bad men from crossin' divide.'

Kirk laughed at that, his eyes bright with merriment.

'You need have no fear of them critturs comin' down off the divide. They fired the valley to scare the hoss, an' were themselves driven from it by a sudden change in the wind that drove the flames towards them.'

'That not good,' the Indian said gravely; and there was concern in his dark eyes.

'Sure it's good,' Kirk interjected suddenly. 'Them cowpunchers, or hoss thieves as they are, must be miles away.... They were driven right out of the valley.'

The Indian was not impressed.

'Which way they go?' he asked abruptly.

'Oh, westward ... towards the big mountains,' Kirk answered.

The fellow raised his hand in salute.

'You follow stallion ... him not yet out of danger. Bad men may come up along river which flows from Raft Mountains. We go so....'

He swung his horse about.

Then half-standing in his saddle, he looked back at Kirk: 'Washakie ... him meet you on trail between Middle and Little Butte in Snake River Plain. Him not forget promise.'

Before Kirk could reply, the Indian gave a sign to his companions and they immediately set off westwards, following the line of the hills from Kelton Pass trail to the Raft River range.

The solitary Indian who had watched Dark Fury and Kirk the previous day had lost no time in gathering together those who had been appointed to ensure the stallion's safe passage into the country of lost rivers.

Meanwhile, Dark Fury was well set on the trail to the northern hill and the river he meant to reach. There was no undue haste in his trotting. Since the Indians had made no attempt to molest him, he knew that they bore him no ill-will. Thus his trotting was again the even pacing of an animal merely intent on travelling on to an already determined rendezvous.

Kirk followed steadily in the direction taken by the stallion. The way was not difficult, going for most of the distance over the sageland. All the while the wooded massif of Black Pine Peak rose up before him, and the gleam of the river took on a scintillating sparkle.

It was evening before he was within a reasonable distance of it and rode at last into the first of the timber adjacent to the mountain.

Dismounting, he led his horse to a stream while he cast around for some trace of Dark Fury. He had not far to look. Some recent droppings were on the trail that led upwards through the trees. He noticed too that it was a clearly marked track, one obviously that had been well used in the past, for it lay like a deep indentation up the hillside.

He decided to follow it first thing in the morning.

Satisfied at the trend of events, he set about lighting a fire and making a suitable camp for the night. At last, with the light gone from the sky and the first stars shining way over the mountain, he sat in silence, watching the occasional movement of his horse beyond the gleam of fire as the animal, hobbled to prevent him straying, cropped the grass. It was still, yet full of all the subtle sounds of the night that did not disturb, but only made the quietness all the more impressive. There was the sibilant murmur of the wind in the trees above his head, the distant cry of an owl, the movement of something among the grass beside the stream. Then the endless play of light and shadow as the moon came up.

The stillness seemed to increase as the hours sped by on soundless feet. It completely enveloped Kirk as he lay unsleeping, his head propped up on his saddle bag. He saw through the interlaced branches of the tree above him the filtering of the moonlight and then the mist of his own breath, silvered on the screen of the invisible air ... silvered to become dissolved, finally lost and gone as his eyes closed in sleep.

Away up on the mountain, Dark Fury was also unsleeping and listening. He sensed an alien taint in the night breezes. ...

Chapter Fifteen

Dawn next day found Dark Fury in a mood of mounting excitement and indecision. He was standing at a point where he could look out towards the west and have an uninterrupted view of the country between Black Pine Peak and the Raft River basin. His nostrils were widely flared as he tested the air streams. The wind, constantly veering from north-west to west, carried a stain he distrusted. All night long he had been aware of that taint. It reminded him, vaguely, of the circus ring from which he had escaped, and with it, the four men who had held him captive.

Dark Fury bristled.

He suddenly understood the warning in the wind. Those same men were coming up out of the west where the Raft River twisted along the plain to join the great Snake River east of Lake Walcott.

In the moment of this realisation, the taint was coming in more strongly on the race of the wind from the west. The stallion became restless and occasionally pawed the ground.

He wanted to be away, moving up the mountain trail to the safety he knew existed up beyond the pine ridge. Yet, he found it difficult to act upon his natural instincts. He was too keenly aware of the fact that down the trail, Kirk Merrett had set up camp. Somehow, he felt he could not travel on without first seeking out the young man's camping site. His curiosity grew stronger with every moment that passed.

At last, although no sign of movement in the plain was visible to cause him alarm, Dark Fury began quite suddenly to move slowly down the trail. The camp was situated farther away than he had anticipated, despite the strong scent of woodsmoke in the air that had intrigued him the previous evening.

The stallion moved quietly. He came upon the camp as Kirk, squatting back on his heels, was cooking his breakfast, his horse, ears pricked, a few yards away.

There was certainly an age-old familiarity in the scene that, in an undefinable manner, Dark Fury recognised. He tossed his head as if irritated at the subconscious probing of small fingers down in the darkness of his animal mind. There was a mild distress in him that he could not readily subdue. The process of trying to recall something that had no direct relationship to him as a living organism was disturbing. He had not the same advantages as that other animal who stood so obviously at ease while his master crouched over a fire of smouldering wood.

Then like a picture suddenly and sharply transmitted on a screen as black as any night, Dark Fury had a glimpse into the past. It was as though he himself had been taken from Black Pine Mountain in Idaho to another pine-clad slope on a mountain high up on the Lemhi Range in the north. This time there was no man squatting back on his heels before a campfire, but a woman. This woman was fair, and her fringed riding habit was as familiar as the hill that slipped down to the valley of the Little Lost River.

Yet it was no woman Dark Fury had ever known, nor yet any woman the great black stallion, his sire, had known. It was, none the less, a woman from out of that shadowland of the long distant past.

Then the miracle of understanding was granted to the stallion as he stood motionless, watching.

The bending shape over the blue-smoked fire appeared to Dark Fury as that of a woman – the very woman who had once known and loved his dam, Firefly; and it was Firefly who had whispered to him out of the past awakening in him this new knowledge of humans, and telling him of the home which once had been hers on the range way up high in the Lemhi Mountains.

So much knowledge was welling up in Dark Fury then, so many

old remembrances that no matter what lay ahead, not altogether would their influences be taken from him. The ancient legend of the Cœur D'Alenes was being revealed to his animal mind, and in that moment, he became the most important part of that legend which had started with his sire, the black stallion, and continued for a short while with his dam, Firefly. ...

... And the stallion, one of the few remaining great horses of the west, sensing that the frost of age was taking toll of his limbs, felt the desire to make one further foray in the Lost River Valley. He quitted the secret canyon by way of the hidden underground trail, and raiding a ranch in the plains, brought one, Firefly, to his hideout under Grouse Creek Mountain. This Firefly was, by nature and breeding, a saddle mare, and after a brief sojourn in the canyon, broke away from the herd and trekked back to her home range where, in the fullness of time, she brought forth her foal who was named Dark Fury by reason of his jet black colouring and unbridled character. ... Dark Fury is the last of the great wild stallions. ...

Thus the legend, created by the Cœur D'Alenes, and often mentioned in the campfire tales of Colorado Ted of Bitter Root, became manifest in Dark Fury himself, not because of the woman Firefly had known, but because the stallion had glimpsed such a shape as she might have presented when he beheld Kirk Merrett on the slope of Black Pine Peak, busy with his morning cooking.

Then because the very intensity of the memory was something he could not bear because it was so close to reality, Dark Fury tossed his head once again, and whinnied sharply.

Kirk looked around. The surprise he experienced was such that he gave a low whistle.

For Dark Fury, however, his moment of remembering was gone, and only the vague, tormenting familiarity of things that had once been remained deep in his animal consciousness. Once more he tossed his head and then, as if he had utterly satisfied his curiosity as regards Kirk's camp, he turned away and went back up the trail. There was a quicker movement now to his pacing, almost as though he felt he must get well on the trail if he were to escape from those whom he knew were his enemies.

He did not glance back to see if Kirk was preparing to follow. He went steadily on, past the look-out post where he had gazed down towards the distant river, pressing on and on until he came out on to the bare scalp of the mountain, and saw the trail winding towards the distant canyons surrounding Deep Creek Peak which was almost halfway to the great falls and the lake north of Wapi. North-east of the lake was Blackfoot and the Big Lost River. . . .

Dark Fury was now bent on reaching Lost Canyon as quickly as possible.

It was well after mid-day before the stallion was able to finally leave the tree-line which, for a considerable distance, had marked the contour of the track. The moment he broke cover, he surprised a cottontail who had crept out of the thicket of trees to nibble the sparse grass.

Although Dark Fury's steps had been muffled on the pine needles, the creature yet heard him approaching, and raised as much as he could his long ears. He looked around, then with a whisk of his scut, he was gone, moving more quickly than any animal the stallion had seen before. A little farther on, under the last sprinkling of small timber, were some sage hens, far from their usual territory, having been driven off by the invasion of some marauding coyotes.

All afternoon, Dark Fury followed the twisting trail that here, on the very shoulder of the mountain, struck due north. The dark and towering shapes of the surrounding hills seemed much nearer than they actually were. In the extreme north, the peaks had the appearance of being more closely massed, the slopes criss-crossed with gulleys and streams, and all but the few lower hills nearer Black Pine Peak, snow clad.

White clouds were flying over the northern plain, and there was moisture in the air. Time and time again did the stallion test it, and always did it seem damp and enervating.

The afternoon waned and died and the sunset was a crimson staining of the cloud masses. When the moon came up and the first stars appeared, they were but shadows of their former glory, for the vapour of the upper air was thickening.

A storm was gathering!

A long way off, a pack of coyotes set up a wailing that fell to a *diminuendo* until it could no longer be heard.

The storm came an hour before daybreak. The moon, having long since foundered amidst the cloud masses, made the hour seem dark indeed. Swiftly then came a rushing wind that brought the vapour masses sweeping over the mountain like smoke. Not many minutes later the rain burst over the peak in a solid wall of water. Far down the mountain, the wind roused a sonorous note from the pine forest.

Dark Fury, standing with his back to the rain, could hear the rising sound reaching up like a thunder of surf on a rocky shore. Soon, the whole mountain resounded to the fury of the storm, the very water gulleys shrieking out as they became filled to overflowing.

At last, the first of the day crept wan and shivering along the eastern horizon, and the stallion, with no protection whatever on the desolate slope, continued to stand like one carved in stone, the rain streaming off his back and forming in an ever-widening pool beneath his feet.

The whole sky above was no more than an expanse of flying vapour, with sometimes a glimpse here and there of heavier clouds shaped in the manner of gigantic birds swooping and rising in the wild race of the wind.

There was no thunder, however. Only the deep-throated note of the wind in the pines some five hundred feet below, and the increasing roar of water pouring down the innumerable gulleys fashioned by the countless storms in the years that had gone.

When, with the passing hours there seemed no sign of the storm abating, Dark Fury wearily set about retracing his steps to the tree-line so that he could obtain a measure of protection under the pines.

An hour or more he took to reach the first of the trees, and it was another hour before he was able to find a satisfactory covering under an ancient yew, little knowing that a hundred yards or so away, Kirk was sheltering under a similar tree.

The storm raged until late in the afternoon when a sullen sunset spread over the summits of the western hills. The clouds began to break up, and only fluttering banners of mist streamed from off the peaks. When at last the moon came up, it soared into a transparent sky, with a bright array of stars in attendance.

Not long afterwards, Dark Fury rousing himself could scent the woodsmoke of Kirk's campfire. Sniffing it, he knew that the young man was close at hand, and for the first time in many hours, he experienced a glow of excitement.

Then because he was still weary and in need of rest, he was no longer aware of the urgency that had sent him heading northwards to Lost Canyon. He therefore sought for, and found, a wallow close to the bole of the tree and lay down in it as a ranch animal might lie in straw. Soon he was asleep. Even so, when a beetle moved slowly over his flank, he swished his black tail to drive the insect off.

A cloud passed over the face of the moon bringing instantaneous shadow to the mountain and an almost impenetrable darkness to the pine forest. A nightbird complained, but ceased when the cloud drifted away and a silver radiance filtered through the trees once more.

Only some frogs croaking in a pool disturbed the silence. Not even the breeze sang in the trees. It had spent itself on the storm that had gone westward. . . .

Chapter Sixteen

The storm, coming as it did so suddenly, was the means of preserving Dark Fury in spite of the discomfort it brought to him. Severe though it was as it swept the slopes of Black Pine Peak, it yet increased in violence as it veered westward to fill and make into a surging torrent the entire watershed of the Raft River.

Luke Unwin and his gang met the full force of the storm as they came around the eastern flank of Cache Mountain. Till then they had followed the watercourse after leaving the ramparts of the Raft River Mountains. Their route had been determined by the knowledge of the locality, and, as the Indians had predicted on their meeting with Kirk, to reach the northern territories – the range of Dark Fury – their best course was to follow the river till it joined up with the Snake River.

They had travelled so rapidly that the Indians failed to pick up their trail until they had gone more than a day's journey northwards.

It was then, with the western slopes of Black Pine Peak falling away in the distance towards the escarpment of Deep Creek Peak that they encountered the full fury of the storm.

Neither Luke Unwin nor Bill Maitland – hardened campaigners in both Nevada and Idaho – had experienced anything like it before. As for the other two, whose ranging area had hitherto been confined for the most part to Wyoming where storms were frequent, the suddenness of the change had been met with indifferent jeering. But when they saw what seemed to be a spiral of grey cloud whirling over the valley, they immediately persuaded the others to make with all speed for safety.

As once before all four had raced before a leaping mass of flame, so now did they race before the advancing spiral of cloud which overtook them just as they were within reach of an outcrop of rock behind which they had hoped to shelter.

What followed was something none of the four men was able to coherently describe. The cloud – the very centre of the storm – had greatly increased as it swept from off Black Pine Mountain, and it seemed to burst asunder over the very heads of the unfortunate men. Maitland was half-lifted from his horse, while Unwin was aware of being thrown forward in the saddle while his crazed animal ran whinneying for the rocks. The other two were a little more fortunate inasmuch as they reached the security of the outcrop, but were badly buffeted and their horses blown against the sandstone formation with a force that made them scream out with pain.

From then on, the rain fell like the fabled deluge that brought destruction to the ancient world. It never ceased for the whole of twenty-four hours, and seemed to be going round and round, and concentrating entirely on the valley between Black Pine Peak and Cache Mountain itself. The men, crouched with their trembling horses behind the sandstone outcrop, were too exhausted to move. As a result, on the last night of the storm, they were unaware that some twenty miles across the valley, the moon was riding high in a sky that, over the opposing mountain in the east, was as clear as any sky in mid-summer.

The nearby river was a raging torrent, and at one point had risen above its banks. It was not until day break that they discovered that they were completely surrounded by a yellow overspill, and that the high ground that supported the rocks had become entirely cut off.

All thoughts of Dark Fury had gone from their minds, and when at last the storm drifted away, they were much too concerned with drying themselves out to trouble about pressing on.

For one whole day and night they remained in the neighbourhood of the rocks, hearing only the roar of the river in full spate, and tormented by the sight of huge herds of deer, driven from their normal grazing grounds by the heavy rain, moving steadily northwards in the direction of those downward thrusting cliffs of the Black Pine Mountain massif.

The four marooned men were forced to live on canned pork and beans, while the best of nature's meat went passing out of sight along the very trail they had hoped to follow themselves.

Once they were disturbed by the hoarse bark of a golden eagle flying high above them. They watched the bird until he went gliding down the airstreams, and in less than thirty seconds, he was miles away, encircling a mountain track where a black stallion was slowly picking his way downhill.

When at last Unwin and his friends hit the trail, they were observed by the Indians, whose skilful tracking no white man could equal.

The Indians acted quickly. Possessing greater knowledge of the locality than the unsuspecting cowpunchers, they rode a little distance into the valley, and then struck off northwards, following a line of small creeks abounding the western slopes of Black Pine Mountain. At the end of the first day's ride, they were in possession of a small canyon up which the gang must ride to hit the northern trail.

It was approaching evening when Unwin and his gang entered the mouth of the canyon, and reconnoitred for a camping site. They found what appeared to be a satisfactory spot, and setting their horses free to graze upon the grassland which hereabouts was plentiful, they set up camp.

All light was slowly drained from the sky, and the moon and stars came out. Coyotes started to yap, having scented the deer which, earlier in the day had reached the grazing grounds frequented by the little yellow wolves.

It was then the Indians began to move in on the four unsuspecting men. Only the restlessness of the grazing horses denoted something untoward taking place in the gloom.

Suddenly a voice, low and compelling, broke the stillness.

'Whitemen better not move!'

'What you want?' Unwin asked sharply, springing to his feet.

There was a brief pause.

'We want nothin' from whitemen,' the Indian replied at last. 'We come only to warn them. Whiteman better leave north trail and go back to desert. Black Stallion not for you.'

At the mention of the stallion, Unwin gave a shout of anger.

'So that's it. ... You're the same crowd that fired ole man Burke's circus, an' stole the hoss. ...'

There was a sinister movement in the gloom beyond the glow of the campfire.

'We no fired circus tepee, nor stole hoss,' the voice came out of the blackness. 'Black Stallion nobody's hoss to steal. Him belong to range.'

With his hand on the butt of his revolver, Unwin asked:

'What if we go north?'

'You not get beyond Snake River.' The Indians voice was menacing. 'The Cœur D'Alenes are a great people, an' they see no harm come to wild hoss. Whitemen best to take warnin' and return to desert trail. ...' The voice paused and then continued, 'Dark Fury not for you, nor for any man. Him under protection of Cœur D'Alenes. We watch every trail north. Remember! You no pass Snake River. This our last warnin'. Whitemen best hold counsel, and go back to south trail. ...'

Unwin peered into the gloom, he thought he saw a movement some little distance away. He called out loudly, defiantly; there was no reply. Only a sage grouse set up its protesting cry.

The trail leading from Black Pine Mountain feel steeply northwards. The massive escarpment of the peak lay far behind. Ahead, the entire continent of rising hills twisted away into affinity, intersected in places by immense canyons with no glimpse of either man or horses to relieve the isolation.

In very truth, Dark Fury's trail to the great Snake River Plain was the loneliest in Idaho.

At night, however, there were indistinct sounds, little scurryings of small animals suddenly come to life in the darkness. There were tiny squeaks, and once, in a stretch of woodland, the sound of crashing branches as a stag thrust his way through the undergrowth in search of a hind. Way out in one of the canyons came the oft-repeated yapping of coyotes on the hunt. . . .

Kirk Merrett was perhaps more aware of these sounds than the stallion who was less than four miles ahead of him. He thought they bore some vague resemblance to the cries of folk lost in the dim corridors of time. The coyotes, in particular, seemed lost to all save themselves and the dim canyons in which they hunted the deer or the elk, or stood cringing beside the rivers where perhaps the rainbow trout leaped in the rapids, or a marauding nightbird swept down on wide-spread wing to snatch a wriggling shape from out of the silver cauldron of some deep pool.

For the first time since he started on the trek, Kirk knew what it was to experience loneliness. It was the loneliness associated with mountains that knew not man, but were of themselves invincible and the homes of creatures who had inhabited them since the world began. . . .

Kirk's evenings were spent in resting against his saddle packs, his feet almost in the grey ash of his campfire; and always did he listen, waiting for the evening sounds to rise up out of the blue haze of distance.

Four days after the storm, Kirk lost Dark Fury's trail. He found himself in an amphitheatre of hills all of which possessed much the same formation and height. Leaving his horse to graze in a hollow, he searched back for some trace of the stallion.

Despite the heavy rain a few days earlier, there was not a single hoofprint save those of his own animal, and no droppings to indicate that he was even on the right track.

That afternoon, Kirk felt more lonely than ever. His blue eyes surveyed each peak in turn; his sun-tanned face began to show signs of strain. He sensed that he had completely lost the animal he had so doggedly trailed from the barren lands of Utah, and now he would never know the secret of Lost Canyon.

Towards evening, he climbed the nearest ridge in an effort to take new bearings. The sunset flared behind him. From the point where Kirk was climbing, the western sky resembled a sea of turbulent gold which was never still, but ebbed and flowed as the glowing sun sank lower and lower towards the mountains and deserts of Oregon.

Kirk felt that when he finally reached the summit of the ridge, he would be able to look out over an area east of that which he sought.

At last he was forced to take a short rest. Breathless, he leant against a boulder. He was thinking how completely desolate these mountains were, and suddenly recalled to mind the Indians he had met when coming down off the pass trail at Kelton.

In a moment his heart contracted. He remembered what their leader had said about Washakie meeting him at Twin Buttes, way out in Snake River Plain.

He almost laughed with relief. Of course! How foolish to have forgotten. That was the route the stallion would surely take to reach the country of the lost rivers. All he had to do was to pick up a sizeable trail likely to lead him out of this mountain wilderness to some watercourse flowing north to the Snake River.

Kirk began to press on up the mountain, and as the last glowing fires of the sunset flickered and went out behind the mountains of the west, he reached the crest of the ridge and started down on the country that lay stretched out on the other side. It was not yet dark, the lower valleys seeming to have caught and retained the last of the day. Then he glimpsed what was clearly a watercourse winding away northwards. Even as his eyes tried to pierce the distance, the light went departing from the valley, and only the twisting streak of the river remained.

Nevertheless, in that brief look over the valley, Kirk had been able to assess the lay of the land. The mountain on which he was standing was broken into a series of canyons a mile or so from the hollow where he intended to camp for the night. The largest of the canyons thrust eastwards to open out on to some scattered clearings that, in turn, gave way to a deep valley that fell steeply in the direction of the river.

He would reach that valley soon after sun-up.

Meanwhile, he started the perilous descent to his camp. The gloom now added to his difficulties, and when he finally reached the lower slopes, he could not locate the hollow where he had left his horse.

Later, he reckoned, he might never have located the horse that night but for the band of coyotes that suddenly invaded the canyon.

The pack came up unobtrusively out of the darkness, running silently after the manner of their near relatives – the grey timber wolves.

They were led by an animal larger than the rest of them, and were bent on rounding up Kirk's horse. Even as they streaked past, running low to the ground, the horse got scent of them and set up a frightened whinney.

This gave Kirk his bearings.

In a split second he was off to protect the horse, and as he stumbled down into the hollow, the first of the coyotes went in to the attack. Fortunately for the horse, the animal jumped a trifle short of his objective, and before he could recover, Kirk, pulling his revolver from its holster, fired a shot into the wriggling body.

Almost before the coyote had given his final kick, Kirk felt the startled movement of the horse beside him. For the very first time since they commenced their travels together, the animal showed what seemed almost a sign of affection for him. He nuzzled his shoulder, and remained close by his side, his body trembling. . . .

After a short while, aware that the coyotes had withdrawn to what they considered was a safe distance, Kirk gathered some dead wood and built up a blazing fire.

Supper that night was a scrambled affair. Kirk kept his rifle handy, while at the same time, making sure that his revolver was fully loaded. You never could tell with coyotes!

After a while he fell into a doze, his eyes wearied by the incessant dancing of the flames. He dreamt that he was no longer there by the fire, but standing out in the glory of a new morning; and in the bright sharp light of sunrise, two immense hills stood out in sharp relief, and between them was a horseman beckoning him on. Beyond the horseman stood something else . . . a black horse . . . Dark Fury!

Kirk felt himself hastening past the one, aware only that he was anxious to reach the great stallion. His teeth were chattering in his eagerness. Then he grew hot; he rolled over on to his side, his head on his arms. . . .

A pain in his left side roused him, and rolling on to his back, he saw, high up, the waning moon sinking like a wrecked galleon over those very peaks that stared down on to the river he hoped to reach next day. He heard his horse munching the grass not far away, and knew that the coyotes had gone despite the fact that the fire was burning low.

He replenished it with further dead wood, and then yawning, stretched out full length beside it and was soon fast asleep.

This time he did not dream. His sleep was profound. He was, for the first time in many days, completely at rest.

Chapter Seventeen

Three days later, full of the confidence of youth, and sure that he was again close on the track of Dark Fury, Kirk Merrett came riding through the gorge between the Deep Creek Mountains and the impressive upthrust of Bannock Peak. The horse's hooves clattered merrily on the loose stones and débris. He tossed his head as he paced evenly along the rutted trail. Like his master, he too had achieved a new confidence which showed clearly in his gait. Every now and again he half turned his head as if trying to get a glimpse of Kirk in the saddle. Since the night of the attack by the band of the coyotes, the animal had developed a strong liking for his master as if he knew that, but for Kirk's timely intervention with the stick that spat fire, he might have joined his late companion in the dark valley of silence.

The trail began to rise, and Kirk, swaying in the saddle, suddenly realised that the gorge was opening out into a clearing where aspens made a glow of whiteness against the red walls of the surrounding cliffs. Striking through the small wood of aspens was a trail of vivid green.

'This is a dandy place to set up camp,' Kirk remarked aloud. 'An early rest 'll do me a power of good fer sure. We've travelled some . . . the hoss an' me. . . .'

He swung himself around and looked back along the trail. All he could see was the grim outline of the mountains that terminated in Deep Creek Peak. Beyond it stretched the endless trail back to Black Pine Peak.

Yep, he thought. He sure had travelled some since coming down off Kelton Pass. He wondered how much farther he would have to go before striking the watershed of the Bannock Range and the foothills marking the course of Snake River.

He straightened himself in the saddle and coaxed the horse to quicken his pace in order to reach the grove of aspens the more quickly. The place seemed tempting, and he sure felt saddle weary.

Acting instinctively, Kirk gave the horse his head, and the animal went off at a swinging trot. Straight towards the trees he went, watching closely the track and fixing every small rise as something he must remember.

He trotted without hesitation to the most likely glade, and without being spoken to, halted and waited for Kirk to dismount. He was growing very wise for a mustang of unknown ancestry, and was learning to interpret his master's wishes.

Kirk's tent was soon erected and the usual fire of dead wood sent its plume of blue smoke unfurling through the trees. Quite near to the camp, a mocking-bird imitated the cry of a solan goose it had heard in the winter. Hidden deep in the wood, a bluebird twittered gaily, and for a long time after he had finished his supper, Kirk lay on his back listening to it, while the darkness crept along the gorge and finally invaded the clearing and the aspen grove.

Not long afterwards, it was another night, as still as had been the countless other nights the clearing had known. The only difference lay in the flickering of the campfire and the slow movement of the horse which grazed under the trees and the man who slept close beside the fire instead of in the tent.

It was the flickering of the camp fire and the scent of woodsmoke carried to them on the breeze that attracted Luke Unwin and his companions.

For many days now, they had followed close on Kirk's trail, and whilst they had no idea as to how near, or far, they were, they knew they were at least travelling in the right direction. In places, hoof prints were more than merely indicated on the track. They were heavily scored, particularly where the ground was moist. The only hoof marks missing were those of Dark Fury. Even so, like Kirk,

Unwin's gang felt they were on the right trail. It was the very route they had followed when bringing the animal down from the desolation of Snake River Plain.

They rode into Kirk's camp a little after midnight, and roused the young fellow by their ribald shouting.

As Kirk sat up, his eyes still heavy with sleep, he heard Unwin remark mockingly: 'Well, if it ain't ole man Burke's buddy. . . . Bet he's after the stallion too.'

The others laughed.

Kirk then saw that all four men were sitting in a half-circle around the fire while their horses stood quietly under the trees.

He strove to speak, but no words came.

'Ain't very entertainin' is 'e?' Maitland remarked, with a vein of sarcasm sharpening the conclusion of the sentence.

'Perhaps ole man Burke told 'im we wuz rustlers or sumthin',' Enos Wills suggested on a wheezing note of laughter.

'Mebbe 'e ain't got a tongue in 'is 'ead anymore,' said Corson, speaking his little piece with obvious relish.

'Cut it out!' Unwin interjected harshly. 'We ain't here for fun.' Then to Kirk, he said slowly, putting a special emphasis on each word: 'Mebbe you can tell us jest where the black stallion is hidin', eh?'

By this time, Kirk had all his wits about him; to save Dark Fury from possible capture by Unwin's gang, he would have to play for time.

He forced a smile to his lips.

'Uh,' he said quickly, 'if I knew jest where the stallion was, I'd hardly be here at me ease in camp. I'd be with him some place back o' the Bannock Range.'

He nodded in a direction well away from the trail he sensed the stallion was following.

'Oh, is that so?' Unwin remarked with a sneer. 'Well, you ain't back o' the Bannock Range, an' never will be. You're right here, kiddo! Mebbe Dark Fury ain't so far either. What 'eve you to say to that?'

He thrust his unshaven chin towards Kirk. In a way, he was

experiencing a sardonic satisfaction in sitting there, leering at the young fellow. All that was brutal in his nature rejoiced in the present situation. He laughed in Kirk's face. Then bending forward, he shook him violently.

'You've no answer to that question, 'eve yeh? We know the hoss is somewhere hereabouts. More'n that, we gotta idea you're all set to meet one of them Indians some place. 'Ow about tellin' jest where, eh?'

Kirk turned his head away from the unshaven chin and beetling brows thrust so close to his face.

Enraged, Unwin caught hold of his hair and forced him to look once again in his direction.

'Quit the stallin'. . . . Where you meetin' that Indian? We know where the redskin is, the stallion won't be far away. Now get talkin'. . . .'

Maitland, Corson and Wills sat motionless, letting Unwin do all the talking. They too were enjoying the situation, each harbouring vivid remembrances of their own unhappy circumstances beside another camp fire.

'I ain't meetin' no Indian,' Kirk managed to gasp.

'What about the hoss?' Unwin probed.

'I ain't seen him since comin' down off the divide from Utah,' he answered.

Unwin's face flushed with increasing rage.

'That's a lie, an' you know it,' he shouted.

'It's the truth,' Kirk reiterated, resolving at all costs not to let Unwin and his gang of ruffians know how well set they were on the stallion's trail.

Unwin's next words, however, confounded him.

'We know the hoss is on this trail, an' hidin' some place near. We brought him along this very trail when we wuz travellin' south to join up with ole man Burke's circus.'

'Then you find him!'

Kirk spat the words out viciously.

Unwin started to laugh again.

'We will! Yeh can be sure of thet. One other thing is certain sure

... you won't! Mebbe we'll leave you here ... tied up, an' easy pickin' fer the coyotes. ...'

He continued to laugh loudly, the others joining in. Unwin then thrust Kirk away from the fire, and sat for a while staring into the flames.

After a few moments of silence, Wills nudged Unwin.

'What we do now, boss?' he asked.

Luke spat into the fire.

'Wait till mornin' ... that's what. We'll settle with this bucko then. Tie 'im up meantime. ...'

Soon afterwards, Kirk, tied hand and foot, lay under the trees, and Unwin and his companions, having eaten their supper, stretched themselves out before the fast-dying fire and dozed.

Kirk knew that it was useless to try and free himself from the bonds. The men were professionals in the making of knots, and they had tied him much too securely to allow for any attempt at escaping. In his despair he was aware of one consolation. His horse had come up from out of the gloom, and stood over him, as if on guard. This seemed to strengthen the feeling of kinship between them, the one attempting to succour the other by nuzzling him. Not till the dawn began to make pink the sky did the animal move off into the trees, and even then, not until he glimpsed the first of Unwin's gang rising to stretch.

Corson cooked breakfast, then all four jested as they ate. They seemed to be in no great hurry to hit the trail.

At last Unwin strolled carelessly over to where Kirk lay.

'Do yeh still say yeh don't know where thet hoss is?' he asked.

Kirk did not answer, but merely glared at his tormenter.

'Oh, well, there's only one way to settle with yeh, me bold kiddo. ...' He looked towards the camp. 'Wills!' he shouted.

Enos Wills was about to obey Unwin's command when Maitland, starting to his feet, pointed upwards.

'Look!' he screamed.

Luke gazed in the direction indicated. His face flushed with excitement.

Way up on a ridge of high ground overlooking the grove of aspens stood Dark Fury. The horse was clearly defined against the red colouring of the cliffs that enclosed the gorge on its eastern limits.

'The stallion!' Unwin shouted hoarsely. 'The black devil himself. . . .'

He ran over to his companions and with them stood staring up at the ledge, mentally debating how best to reach it and drive the stallion into some broken gorge from which he could not escape.

It dawned on him then that the ledge could not be reached from this side of the valley. A steady focusing of his eyes on the cliff disclosed the fact that the ledge was part of a seam in the rock which began where a break in the mountain showed clearly where a divide led down to the opposite side of the range.

All four men had completely forgotten Kirk. They continued to stare unfalteringly at the motionless shape of the horse that seemed so near and yet so far away.

'We'll heve to make fer the divide,' Unwin began.

His voice died in his throat as a sharp cry came echoing down from the ridge. It went on and on in what seemed a rising note of excitement.

Willis had ceased to stare up at the stallion. Something in the stallion's stance caused him to glance up at the head of the gorge.

He gave a shout of warning.

'The Indians. . . . They're headin' this way. . . .'

The others reached for their guns as they took in the scene at a glance. Wills was right. The band of Cœur D'Alenes had indeed entered the gorge, and although still more than a mile away, were riding towards the aspen grove.

'We'll fight it out,' Unwin cried.

Wills shook his head.

'We'd better make a getaway while the goin's good. There's too many of them. They'd finish us off sure. If we get out of the gorge, we might yet get the hoss. 'E ain't thet far away!'

Unwin, for all his blustering, was not slow in agreeing with Will's observations. There was no time now to decide what to do with their captive as the Indians were approaching very rapidly. They resolved to leave him where he was.

'Let his pals see to him,' was Unwin's comment as he and the others hastily saddled their horses.

'How about this?' Maitland said, indicating his gun.

Unwin shook his head.

'Them Indians 'ud 'eve another score to settle with us then, an' we might never get the hoss. ...'

He jumped up into the saddle as he spoke.

The gang rode off just as the Cœur D'Alenes entered the first of the timber and headed direct for the camp.

Kirk, unable to suppress the excitement he felt, lay waiting for the help he knew now was approaching. He swore to get even with Unwin, whatever the cost. He struggled into a sitting posture stirred by the violent surging of emotion in his breast, and saw the Indians riding up the grassy trail between the aspens.

What he did not see was the shape of Dark Fury still up on the ridge watching every movement of both friends and enemies.

The stallion remained unmoving until the Cœur D'Alenes halted before the remains of Kirk's camp fire while two of their number, dismounting, hastened to release the young man from his bonds.

Then, and only then, did Dark Fury leave this vantage point so high above the valley, making with unerring instinct for the divide from which a well-defined trail led down to Silver Creek and the tributary that flowed direct to the distant Snake River. ...

Chapter Eighteen

The ground in silver creek had dried up, and despite the heavy rain of a few days before, the river was running quite low. A woodpecker drummed loudly on a decayed oak tree that still continued to grow gnarled and twisted close to the track Dark Fury was following. The bird ceased when it beheld the stallion, and stood clinging precariously to the bark of the trunk with head turned to one side so that it could better observe the approach of the animal who had suddenly invaded this hitherto undisturbed hinterland of the mountains.

Dark Fury paused close to the old tree and then went slowly to the river to drink.

The woodpecker continued to watch him, and only fluttered to a higher position when a porcupine moved swiftly across the trail to the security of a boulder. But for the movement of the porcupine, and that of the stallion, there was nothing else in the entire wood to cause the woodpecker alarm.

Dark Fury was conscious of the quietness as he dipped his muzzle into the river to drink. It reminded him of many another such quietness that he had known in other remote places. Here, not even the murmuring of the tumbling currents seemed to touch his hearing. He only knew that the river was flowing endlessly on, moving in one long silver gleam that broke into arrow-heads of light where shallows marked the watercourse.

Then again the drumming of the woodpecker on the old tree trunk went echoing up into the still air. The sound and the gleaming flow of the river seemed to be one. Dark Fury was no more aware of one than he was of the other.

Nature, in Silver Creek, was a kindly thing, so different from the dangers he had known since his escape from the showground. The stallion was almost inclined to stay awhile beside the river.

Already he had made a distinct classification of events. He knew that danger such as he had experienced in the past existed for the most part only in the nearness of the four men who had originally taken him captive. For those others, the Indians and Kirk, he had no feeling of fear. He was beginning to accept them as followers habitual to the trail. If anything, he sensed a special affinity with Kirk, born out of what the young fellow had done for him, and strengthened by his persistence in keeping so close to him on the trail.

Even as these vague glimmerings of what was instinctive reasoning passed through his brain, Dark Fury experienced once more the more urgent growth of curiosity taking possession of him. As a result, when glancing back along the trail, he half expected to see Kirk riding towards him.

At last, moved by the intensity of the reactions he began to experience, the stallion moved from the river to stand for some minutes beside the old tree where, once again, the woodpecker clung very quiet and very still, watching him.

Dark Fury was conscious of a strange disappointment when, after some little while, no sign of Kirk was visible on the distant approaches of the trail.

By this time, the afternoon sun was deepening in shade and on one peak where snow lay in heavy drifts, the colour slowly expired like a flame dwindling and dying in a place where winds held constant play. Mauve-blue contours marked the division between earth and sky. Lower down, the contours merged into one like hands folded across a breast of snowy whiteness. They did, however, but serve to foreshorten the serrated outline of the unnamed peak that rose in the east, lost in a halo of cloud.

Whilst Dark Fury continued to stand gazing up the trail, he did not observe the constant change of colour on the mountains, but did see the shadows lengthening across the river; and a wind coming from off the unnamed peak blew over him in a steady stream, and fanned his long black tail until it waved slowly like a silken banner.

It was then, perhaps, more than at any time since his escape from Burke's corral that Dark Fury seemed again to be in his full prime. Despite his journeying, and the hardships he had undergone, the leanness had gone from his frame, and his hide had taken on a new lustre that was the lustre of good health. He had assuredly recovered from his desert ordeal. His intelligence too had sharpened in that he was able to assess more quickly the dangers that might threaten him from the approach of those who, in the past, had betrayed him. He possessed also a more reactionary method of reasoning, closely allied to a new courage that was born of new experience rather than of the wild. Moreover, he was thrilled with the sense of well-being that moved through him like the surging of a warmer blood through his veins.

With his head set high on his sturdy neck, and his black tail being gently fanned by the rising breeze, he might have been in very truth the black talisman of the Cœur D'Alenes waiting for the great chieftain to come and sit astride his gleaming back.

For ten minutes, maybe fifteen, he stood thus under the shadow of the decaying oak tree, while less discernible shadows continued to lengthen across the river, and the mauve-blue contours of the hills far up the valley became misted over with a scarf of cloud that had unfurled from off the unnamed peak.

Then, the stallion was no longer there. He had departed suddenly, travelling swiftly westwards; and only the woodpecker saw him depart. It seemed that the lengthening shadows pursued him like transient range followers who sought quickly to reach that strange country beyond the Snake River Plain.

By the time the woodpecker had resumed its monotonous drumming, light was departing from the river and the westering sun sinking behind the ramparts of the hills that kept the Oregon State Line.

Dark Fury, in crossing over the hill track that led away from the valley of the aspens, did not follow the main trail leading down to the river basin. Instead, he turned into a small creek that struck north-wards and was concealed by the walls of the main mountain ridge that followed the watercourse that shaped the valley west of the Bannock Range.

This unexpected move by the stallion had thrown Luke Unwin and his gang completely off his track. Unsuspecting his change in tactics, they had followed the main trail which they had used when they had captured Dark Fury.

Kirk Merrett was more fortunate inasmuch that after he had been released by the Indians, they had agreed to accompany him as far as the Snake River Basin. Thus when the young man and the Cœur D'Alenes came out on to the mountain trail, and saw the small northward creek, one of the Indians investigated the ground very carefully, finally remarking with calm assurance that Dark Fury had, at this point, deserted the main track and had gone due north.

This caused the leader of the Cœur D'Alenes to reconsider his previous decision to accompany Kirk as far as the Snake River. His task was to keep in close touch with Luke Unwin and his companions who had clearly kept to the main trail.

He consulted the remainder of the band.

It was well past noon when the Cœur D'Alenes indicated that because of Dark Fury's deviation, Kirk would have to travel alone up the creek in search of the stallion. As the leader explained, Dark Fury was Kirk's responsibility whereas Luke Unwin and his dis-reputable friends were his.

'We keep bad men on move,' the leader said.

Kirk understood, and while thankful for what the Cœur D'Alenes had already done for him, was secretly overjoyed to know that he was to journey on alone. He had long since discovered that he preferred his own company to that of others. There was, he often confessed to himself, a strange delight in travelling alone, for it gave one much time for thinking and searching out the secret places of the heart. Moreover, alone, one got to savour the atmosphere of a place and to know that it was not merely an expanse of country made up of just so many hills and valleys.

Kirk, like many another man before him, was not long in discerning that there were sermons a-plenty to be read in stones, and the whole history of the world in the shape of a mountain or in the burrowing of a watercourse. What was more, one learnt these things quickly when one had time and silence in which to pause and reflect. . . .

His smile of assent satisfied the Cœur D'Alenes who, raising their hands in token of farewell, spurred their horses forward. They went down the mountain trail at a steady trot leaving Kirk free to pursue his solitary way along the creek that, within a few miles, opened out on to the fair prospect of Silver Creek.

Like Dark Fury, Kirk too was feeling exceedingly fit. His brief encounter with Luke Unwin's gang had done little more than rouse in him the desire to get even at some future date. For the rest, he was happy to be in the saddle, listening to his horse's feet clip-clopping along the trail, and knowing that no matter what happened now, there must come the day when he would be safely across the Snake River and in the great plain itself; and then, in a month, mebbe two, would be in the land of the lost rivers and at not too great a distance from Lost Canyon.

Kirk thought a lot about Lost Canyon that afternoon. Indeed, it occupied most of his conscious thinking from the very moment he left the Cœur D'Alenes. It was not, after all, entirely in a spirit of adventure that he wanted to visit the hidden canyon, nor was it altogether because it was Dark Fury's legendary home. He really wanted to discover if the old tales about it were true . . . whether, as was so often said by old timers, it was a valley rich in gold desposits. Also – and despite Dark Fury, this it was that thrilled him the most – whether it was indeed the last stronghold of the great wild horse bands.

With the night already heavy on the hills, he entered the approaches of Silver Creek. The silence was unbroken; not even the woodpecker drummed where the old oak tree was like a crooked shadow down on the trail.

Reining his horse, Kirk sat hunched in the saddle, trying to catch some faint movement or sound.

He drew in his breath as he felt a wild elation rising up in him. Once more he realised that this was truly the life all men should live. The faint gleam of the river that was like a silken thread slipped quietly away to the unending plain of Snake River. Suddenly, he heard a night bird call out clear and strong, and the sound was like music in his ears, reaching up and entwining itself about his heart.

Some little time later when he rode down towards the twisted shape of the ancient oak, he knew from some very recent droppings that here it was Dark Fury had been but a few hours before.

In spite of the old familiar thrill he experienced at the discovery, it was important that he should set up camp and rest his horse awhile. The animal had been constantly on the move since leaving the aspen grove early that morning.

One consolation Kirk had, however. Even as he and his own horse must rest, so indeed must the stallion take rest, and the miles that separated them would not be materially lengthened by the night that must pass before he again broke camp and hit the trail.

It was as he dismounted and prepared to erect his tent by the oak tree that Kirk heard the first frail shiver of the river. It crept up to him from out of the gloom, a sharp musical murmur where the currents eddied over some broken shallows.

The sound was, for all the world, like a complaint in rhythm – a complaint, moreover, that rose and fell, reached a sharp-edged note of pain, then subsided. It might have been the old eternal cry of the river for the warmth and light that evening had taken away. There might have been a mild resentment in it too, a resentment of the loneliness that night brought when the wind blew chill from off the mountains, and only the stars quivered like drowned things in the deep pools where the rainbow trout were wont to lie.

Because of it, Kirk had the feeling that Silver Creek in being so intimate had accepted him, and that he could rest the night in peace without fear of being overtaken by those who, the previous night, had come upon him unawares.

Even as the river predicted, only the wind stirred as he slept, the chill wind the river had always known. At daybreak, the woodpecker was back at its drumming in the oak trunk, and out in the river, a trout leaped, and way up above the mountain peaks, a wide-pinioned eagle came gliding down the uncharted airlines of the sky. . . .

Yes, indeed! Life was truly a thing of never-ending surprises and beauty to one travelling alone!

Book Four
Lost Canyon

Chapter Nineteen

The Snake River was entirely different from any river Kirk had yet seen in his travels. There was no clearly marked trail following the course of the great river, and no causeway that he could see likely to aid him in crossing over the opposite bank. He was not so long in arriving at the conclusion that he would have to journey eastwards in search of a likely place to enable him to make the crossing with any degree of safety. Moreover, such a spot as he had in mind would have to be substantially constructed, for the river flowed rapidly, and where not boulder-strewn, was of considerable depth. He also noticed that where it wound around an occasional bluff, it went in a wide loop, the currents appearing to flow swifter as if caught up in a whirlpool that boiled and steamed as it sped in increasing violence away from the bluff and into the greater flow of the main stream.

Kirk noted that the immediate formation of the river basin was, for the most part, gravelly, with here and there heavy banks of silt, obviously deposited in times of heavy flood.

Thus, Kirk had no difficulty in picking up the first real traces he had of Dark Fury since leaving Silver Creek many days before.

Hoof marks were scored in neat precision all along the bank, going in an east to north-easterly direction. Dark Fury too, was obviously seeking a place by which he could reach the opposite shore with safety.

On that first day of his arrival in the vicinity of the river, Kirk found himself gazing long and often at the wide green plain that stretched away beyond the limits of the river's northern bank. It seemed to go on and on in a swelling sea of green, with here and there the scarlet hue of the Indian paint-brush vying with the almost startling magenta of cactus. Far over, however, he could see where the plain, a darker green, vanished into the half-blue gloom of ravines that thrust down upon it from the vast volcanic outpourings many miles north of which the famous Craters of the Moon were but a small part.

A stranger though he was to Idaho, Kirk knew at once that way out beyond the confines of the Snake River Plain lay the world's most desolate country – the Jurassic uplift with its innumerable folds in the earth's surface, and its enormous granite gorges and basaltic buttes.

With this realisation biting deeply into his mind, he felt like one who, having already travelled an immense distance, was yet faced with a more exacting journey, and this time, not a journey across a vast uncharted desert, but across a land of mystery where were gathered all the remaining wild animals who sought protection from man in a place where man seldom came.

Even here, the tranquillity of the desert and of Silver Creek was no longer evident. The river lifted up its voice in a never ending chorus. It seemed also possible that even when across on the opposite bank and riding out into the plain, there would always be sound and movement following Kirk. That world he glimpsed way off there was vaster than anything he had yet encountered, and so it would be until he came at last to the valley of the lost rivers and Dark Fury's home range.

Yet in spite of the many obvious difficulties that lay before him in his quest, Kirk was in no way dismayed. It was thus with a smile that he set up camp for the night close to the first bluff he encountered and within full sound of the toss of the river as it whirled on its way to the great lake and canyons that lay many miles to the north-east.

Next day Kirk was off with a grim determination to find some way to cross the river and, if possible, to choose the very same spot taken by Dark Fury.

The stallion's footprints were still clearly discernible for many of the miles Kirk traversed that day. Indeed, he only lost sight of them when he hit an area composed entirely of broken rock and enormous slabs clearly of volcanic origin.

It was well towards the heel of the day before he finally reached a spot where immense granite ridges broke the surface of the river. At first sight, it seemed that at one or two points they might serve as a possible means of reaching the opposite shore. The only real obstacle, as far as Kirk could see, was a narrow channel that intersected the ridges about halfway across and carried the full flow of the currents.

Confident, however, that the channel was not likely to present any great difficulty, Kirk decided, in view of the rapidly fading light, to wait for the morrow before making up his mind.

As the night shadows dropped down, his camp fire again sent its haze of blue smoke spiralling up into the air. There was no wind to send it drifting across the river or the plain; and it might indeed have been an Indian smoke signal so straight did it rise above the river basin.

This time it did not attract any but one solitary creature who stood high up on a slope of bare rock where he could survey the entire course of the river and the land that lay adjacent to it.

It was Dark Fury, still on the south bank of the great Snake River.

The stallion moved down off the escarpment when it was quite dark, and trod so silently that not even a stone was loosened by his hooves as he made towards Kirk's camp.

Although he was well familiar with this place, Dark Fury had, for some obscure reason, been reluctant to press on across the river. Somehow, he had sensed from the very moment he left Silver Creek that Kirk was not far behind him on the trail, and that soon they must meet.

Dark Fury scented Kirk's horse when still some little distance away, and he cast about in a half-circle until he was able to approach the camp from a less conspicuous angle.

That night, the stars burned brightly in a sky of almost liquid purple, and in places found reflection in the deep pools that lay quietly where immense rocks afforded protection from the swiftly flowing currents of the main stream.

For more than an hour, Dark Fury stood like a statue, savouring once again the pleasing sensation of gazing upon the flickering glow of the camp fire and knowing that Kirk was sleeping before it. As once before, he was aware of the vague familiarity of things that had not been of his ken, but of another. The singing in his blood stirred into restless movement those things of the past that, for him, had no direct connection with anything he had known. Yet, as he stood there watching, they seemed to become stronger than any experiences he had yet known in his long career in the wild.

The last stars were fading like the embers in the fire when Dark Fury finally made his way back to the escarpment. He went zig-zagging between the scant tracks of green reaching at last the yellow gravel below the rocky formation. There he stood looking back, but made no attempt to retrace his footsteps when he saw the spiral of smoke from the fire suddenly increase as Kirk, having awakened early, prepared to make his breakfast.

An hour later the young man had once again broken camp, completely unaware that Dark Fury was so close. Not long afterwards, Kirk ws investigating the river and the granite ridges, seeking out the best route by which he could cross to the northern bank without mishap to either himself or his horse.

Kirk selected the longest and widest of the ridges for his venture, and gathering together the first of his many packs, he started to carry it across to the other bank. His first journey, understaken with so little knowledge of the hazards likely to impede his progress, seemed easy enough, and the channel through which the river flowed seemed less turbulent than he had imagined.

His second attempt with another pack of similar size, was not so easily accomplished. For a reason he could not determine, the flow of water through the channel was swifter, and there appeared to be a decided tug in the undercurrent. Moreover, he felt he could discern an ominous rumble from up river, little understanding that the sound was actually carried from far downstream where, hidden by a bend, the river hurtled through a narrow ravine. The undertow Kirk found so disturbing was a returning current caught by the main stream fifty yards or so above the rock ridges and there turned back to swell the flow of water through the channel.

This movement of the undercurrent had been absent on the first occasion because a fall of stones had temporarily checked the returning intake.

Even so, Kirk felt that he could finally lead his horse over to the opposite bank without mishap since there would be no saddle packs for the animal to carry.

It was clear, however, that the horse himself did not view the river with any sign of approbation. He constantly tossed his head and rolled his eyes. None the less, he had long since come to trust his master, and when Kirk took hold of the bridle, he followed quietly enough.

There was not the slightest doubt the crossing would have been made without any trouble whatever but for the fact that when both man and horse reached the channel, a piece of heavy driftwood came floating towards them.

This unexpected movement on the surface of the river startled the horse and he pulled against the bridle.

Kirk spoke soothingly, but in vain.

The driftwood, like an overturned canoe, suddenly rose, end upwards, swinging a little towards the granite ridge causing the horse to panic. In a moment he had pulled himself free of Kirk's hold, and slithering on the ridge, was himself in the water, and being forced down the channel towards the point where the rock ridges ceased and only the open river flowed surging between widely separated banks.

Kirk with a cry of surprise, thrust after the struggling animal.

What confidence he had, received a severe check when he also found himself caught by the sudden turn of the current, and battling along behind the driftwood which was now harrying the horse as it rose and fell upon the breaking tide-race.

There was no time to make sudden decisions. Kirk could only

155

struggle on. The river was full of a wild defiance, seemingly intent on drowning both horse and man.

Meanwhile, the horse had been thrust out of the channel into the wider expanse of the river. The currents were stronger than ever and sweeping him along. Here and there whitened runs of water told of sudden rapids; at other points, the water seemed gathered into one immense pool of unimaginable depths.

Kirk by this time was swimming with the current, and treading water for an instant, shouted loudly to the horse who, at the sound of his master's voice, endeavoured to turn towards him.

In so doing, his hooves managed to grapple for a few short seconds a stretch of gravel, and there he stood, terror-stricken, but vaguely aware of the approach of his master on an incoming surge of water.

Not a moment too soon did Kirk reach the gravel bar and grasp the trailing rein. In the instant his fingers closed over the leather, the driftwood, caught in a sudden eddy, came flowing back under the horse's feet.

With a neigh of dismay, the animal reared, pulling Kirk into the very centre of the gravel bed.

Gritting his teeth, Kirk tried to regain some sort of foothold, did indeed manage to mould his body into a firm enough stance to withstand the pull of the tide-race. Then, with the driftwood once again caught by a firm downstream current and floating crazily away, Kirk stood gripping the bridle and speaking sharply to the horse in an effort to distract him from the surging break of the water.

For fully three minutes he stood helpless on the gravel bar, and all the while the horse kept tossing his head.

Then before the animal could quite grasp what was happening to him, Kirk was on his back, and he felt himself being urged out into the race of the river, the very thrust of his master's body instinctively guiding him to the opposite bank.

The swift surge of the river broke and fell against his flanks. It seemed to the terrified animal that the very boulders were shaking in the renewed impetus the torrents were making to sweep both him and his rider around the bend of the watercourse and so into the ravine where the spin of the currents resembled a whirlpool.

Kirk used all his reserves of strength to keep the horse moving against the pull of the currents.

'Up!' he shouted repeatedly, and each time he spoke, the horse half rose in the water, only to strike out with increased vigour the instant he felt the tug of the bridle lessen as his master sought to aid him in his efforts.

At last the fight with the river was at an end. The northern shore was scarcely five yards distant.

Kirk then made another surprising move. He slid off the animal's back and literally hurled himself towards the bank while yet retaining his grip on the rein.

The horse was propelled along after the hunched shape of his master, and a second later stood trembling on what was little more than a gravelly foreshore, barely touched by the ebb and flow of the currents.

Breathless, Kirk looked back up the river. He experienced yet another shock. The struggle had taken him more than a mile from the point where he had deposited the saddle bags.

Undaunted, he led the now chastened horse to a stretch of grazing, and leaving him, went striding back along the bank, regardless of his dripping clothes and the fact that he was shivering in the sudden drive of the wind from off the distant ravine.

It was late afternoon before he got another camp set up and a huge fire burning brightly. He began to realise how near he had been to losing the horse, and perhaps his own life in the bargain.

Sufficient for the day, however, the tribulations he and the horse had endured.

He would spend the evening taking his ease. Even so, the thought persisted in his mind that the way to Lost Canyon was certainly not without its hazards. This fact was more than ever impressed on him when, on the incoming wind, he heard more clearly than ever the heavy rolling of the river over rapids that were confined between high walls of rock. He hoped the Snake River Plain and the granite gorges and basaltic buttes would not present greater difficulties.

Again the vague thought chasing through his mind ... sufficient for the day. ...

That night he slept the sleep of the just. No thought moved in the darkened mirror of his mind, and when morning came, he awakened like one ready to conquer the whole world!

Chapter Twenty

The morning that saw Kirk Merrett awakening like one ready to conquer the world was a morning particularly memorable in the life of the stallion, Dark Fury. Just before the sun came up, shadows covered the many hollows surrounding the area of the Snake River basin. Thus no movement was visible in the dim half-light that was spilling over the mountains of the east.

Dark Fury had slept the whole night through standing against an overhang of the very rock that did service as a look-out post. He had witnessed Kirk's desperate struggle to cross the river, and had followed the young man almost as far as the ravine. Then when Kirk had succeeded in making the crossing with his horse, Dark Fury had returned to the rock conscious that soon now he too, would be fording the river so as to reach that more familiar country adjoining his home range.

He was wiser than Kirk in that he knew the exact place to attempt the crossing. It was in fact a gravel bar that extended most of the way to the opposite bank, and for countless centuries had been in constant use by those animals trekking from north to south or, as in Dark Fury's case, trekking from south to north. The bar was situated close to the ravine and at not too great a distance from the point where Kirk had struggled hard to get his horse to safety. As in the case of the granite ridges farther up river, channels were scored in the gravel, but all narrower than the one that had all but brought disaster to Kirk's horse.

Not only was Dark Fury aware of this traditional fording bar of Snake River, but the Cœur D'Alenes too, knew of it. Luke Unwin was also familiar with it, for had not he and his friends brought Dark Fury across it on the occasion of the long journey southwards to meet up with Burke's Circus in Utah?

During the past few days Unwin's gang had been uneasily conscious of the Indians close on their heels. Hoping to shake them off, they had struck the river basin at a point where heavy timber had given them a measure of covering. As a result, the Cœur D'Alenes had temporarily lost touch with them. Finding no trace of the gang in the vicinity of the river, the Indians took a more easterly trail, and kept close watch on the gravel bar from a camp set up amongst the crags of the ravine.

Unfortunately for Dark Fury, he was nearer to Unwin's gang than he was to those who were anxious to preserve and assist him on his trek back to Lost Canyon. Moreover, that last night he spent on the south bank of the river was one during which he slept more soundly than usual.

It was the unaccustomed screaming of a loon and the distant yammer of a coyote that roused him into a nervous awareness of something happening in the grey light of dawn. Then because the sounds were not repeated, he started to graze where he stood, and it was fully an hour later when he climbed up on to the summit of the rock to make one last survey of the territory he was bent on quitting.

Then he saw them – Luke Unwin and his three motley henchmen – all industriously following the same trail that Kirk Merrett had followed the previous day.

'The stallion! The stallion!' Wills was the first to raise his voice, and Dark Fury could hear the sound of it even from where he stood.

Every outline of him was etched against the primrose gold of the sky. His dark tail seemed to be moving gently in the rising breeze. He screamed his defiance at them raising his head so that the call could break easily from his throat. Loud and clear it drifted down to them, harsher than on that other occasion when he had screamed at them. All four had the uncomfortable feeling that this time the stallion was threatening them.

'He's sure sum mad,' Maitland whispered.

'It's not fer long he'll be roamin' the plain, an' he knows it,' Unwin answered. 'Mebbe it's thinkin' he is that this is his last day of freedom. ...'

Then without warning, he lashed his horse into a sudden gallop, and pulling his lariat free, went whooping up the trail, leaving his three confederates to follow as best they could.

For a minute or more, Dark Fury stood motionless on his look-out post, watching the approach of the four men he hated most in all the world. Then he uttered one further scream which brought a response from the loon far up river and a slow lament from the coyote way out in the timberland.

Before the coyote's mournful cry had died away into silence Dark Fury was moving cautiously down off the rock, and reaching firm ground, struck off eastwards in order to follow a gravel watercourse that went like a yellow gash to the very summit of the cliffs forming the ravine through which the river flowed.

Only one idea was in the stallion's mind now. He sensed that Unwin and his followers would forestall any attempt he might make to cross the Snake River by way of the gravel bar. Thus he made without hesitation straight for the awesome cliffs that rose some two hundred feet and gradually narrowed until the river, far below, rushed boiling and rumbling through a gulley little more than ten feet wide.

By this time, others were aware of Dark Fury's great effort to once again elude the machinations of Luke Unwin. The Cœur D'Alenes had caught but the faintest echo of the stallion's scream of defiance; but the sound had alerted them. They rode out from their secret hiding-place amidst the crags and hit the river trail some four hundred yards east of the gravel bar. They also were of the opinion that Dark Fury was heading for this most ancient of fording points.

Kirk Merrett, till then, unsuspecting of the great events that were in the making on the south bank of the river, was about to start his long trek northwards when he saw first the Cœur D'Alenes, then riding full towards them, Luke Unwin and his gang.

Unwin, still well in the lead, saw the oncoming Indians too late to break the pace he was making. He was forced to swing completely away from the trail, at the same time endeavouring to warn his friends.

His horse stumbled at the unexpected swerve, throwing him from the saddle. Scrambling to his feet Luke made for the nearest boulder, pulling his revolver from its holster. As the Indians approached, he fired.

Then he was aware that he had been joined by the rest of his gang, and all four fired shot after shot on the now scattering band of Cœur D'Alenes.

'Keep it up, fellers!' he urged, encouragingly; then to his dismay, realised that the band was scattering not because of the shots, but with a view to encircling them.

Struggling to his feet, he shouted: 'Make fer the hosses. . . .'

He jumped away from the boulder and ran for his horse, closely followed by the others.

In a matter of seconds they were galloping back along the trail, hotly pursued by the Cœur D'Alenes who seemed more anxious to drive them from the river basin than to kill them.

The four men, however, felt that their only salvation lay in reaching the heavy belt of timber that had given them protection over the past couple of days.

Kirk, a startled witness of the short combat and pursuit, felt that the Cœur D'Alenes were unaware of his presence on the northern bank of the river. They gave no sign as they raced along the southern trail after the fleeing horses thieves.

Realising that there was no real assistance he could render the Indians, and that with Unwin so close on his heels, it was necessary to locate Dark Fury as quickly as possible, he decided to ride off north.

He might never have seen the stallion that day but for the fact that as he headed his horse away from the river, his eyes for a brief moment encountered the hummocky ground rising steeply towards the head of the ravine.

Dark Fury had, by this time, come up out of the gravel water-course and was making for the very summit of the ravine. He was moving swiftly, startled by the shots and not knowing that the Cœur

D'Alenes were driving Unwin and his men back along the river trail.

Kirk's surprise was manifest in the gasp of astonishment that came from his lips. Coupled with it was a sense of awe, for on following the contour of the cliff he saw where the river narrowed and went thundering through the two opposing escarpments.

He immediately set his horse's head in the direction of the ravine in his desire to keep Dark Fury in sight. Even then, as the stallion forged steadily on, there was no thought in Kirk's mind as to the animal's intentions. He was certainly unprepared for what was soon to follow.

As he rode a straight course up the northern slope of the ravine, he was greatly astonished at the tremendous changes taking place in the scene with every yard he travelled. The ground was thrust up into a similitude of mounds, crags and wind-swept buttes. These, however, were but minor folds in the earth's surface when compared to the summit of the gorge which went curving away in a winding line that turned back on itself and then went sweeping on again, keeping the raging torrent confined some two hundred feet below.

All the while, Kirk could see the stallion on the southern cliff thrusting up higher and higher until he began to realise that the distance between the two cliffs was lessening, and then that the river was threshing through a gorge that was full of spray very like purple smoke rising up from out of the hidden depths.

Kirk pulled his horse to a sudden halt. It was beginning to dawn on him that Dark Fury's determined ascent to the summit was not without reason. His heart missed a beat. Surely the stallion was not going to attempt a leap from one cliff to the other?

Panic rose up in him at the thought.

'No! No!' he cried in sudden alarm.

Kirk then became aware of the deep-throated roar of the river tossing and tumbling in the cleft far below. With one eye still on the stallion, he dismounted and crept towards the edge of the cliff. He drew back with a sharp cry of fear. All he could see was a dark vent with a ragged wall that bulged outward as if to hide the river. The spume rose like steam into his face. A little farther on, it still possessed the colour of purple smoke twisting and turning in the air.

Then he forgot the gorge and the rising spray; as his gaze became fully concentrated on Dark Fury. It seemed to him that the stallion was at last conscious of his presence on the opposite cliff.

For an instant the horse stared full at him, panting with the exertion he had made to reach this spot so high above the river he would cross.

'No!' Kirk screamed to him across the gap. 'Go back!'

But Dark Fury could not hear him above the thunderous roar of the torrent.

A moment longer did the stallion stand staring at him. Then his neck thrust out, reminding Kirk of the hideous creature he had rescued from the swamp. There was the same primeval look about the half-snarling lips, the same vicious gleam of teeth.

The stallion's legs suddenly doubled up beneath him. Every vein in his body stood out so clearly that even from where he stood, Kirk could see them pulsing and throbbing with suppressed vitality.

A second passed ... maybe two. ...

Dark Fury's stance was firmly established!

Then like a thunder-bolt, he leapt forward. His dark body went hurtling across the gap, to become partially obscured for an instant in the haze of purple vapour that whirled up about him like a garment tossed up by the river to clothe him.

No cry; no leap so foreshortened as to send the stallion crashing down to his death in the torrent two hundred feet below. All Kirk saw was the sudden blending of vapour and cloud, and emerging from them like a winged horse of some ancient legend ... Dark Fury!

Then, and only then as his feet touched that northern cliff, did Dark Fury send a mocking scream resounding down the ravine to die in pealing echoes as it passed from wall to wall.

When Kirk turned to go back to his horse, his limbs were weak. He felt sick.

Of Dark Fury, however, nothing save his leaping shape travelling north to that hinterland of lost rivers where lived others like himself. ...

Chapter Twenty-one

As Kirk Merrett set out into the fastnesses of Snake River Plain, following doggedly the trail already set by Dark Fury, he little guessed how great an adventure this last part of the journey was going to be. All that had happened to him since that morning when he left Burke's Circus in Utah to brave an uncharted desert, was of small importance against the mighty issues that awaited him beyond the confines of the Big Butte country. He knew that the farther north he went, the hazards of making a safe trek would increase. Beyond the Big Butte country lay the desolate area of the Lost River Sinks which, in an age long gone, had swallowed up the rivers that had come gushing down from out of the immense mountain ranges.

Nevertheless, despite this knowledge, Kirk felt quite at ease as he rode out into the plain. He was confident that where Dark Fury went, he could most certainly follow. Moreover, he knew for certain now that the stallion was not heading north without a definite purpose.

Washakie had spoken of the Twin Buttes, and Kirk sensed that the stallion was making in just that direction. Somewhere, out beyond the buttes in the neighbourhood of the mountains and valleys of the lost rivers, was the secret canyon.

Kirk thrilled to the sound of the name. Secret Canyon! Lost Canyon!

Merrett drew himself erect in the saddle with a sense of pride at having come so far on the trail. All the difficulties Burke had mentioned had been overcome; he had even been instrumental in saving

Dark Fury from a terrible death. His only regret was that he had lost his other horse on that treacherous mountain trail way back in the borderland territory. Still, he had been lucky inasmuch that the better animal of the two had survived the many dangers of both mountain and river, and now, at long last, he was setting out across the Snake River Plain towards the buttes and Lost Canyon!

Again he thrilled to the name, murmuring it to himself over and over again. It was sure a grand soundin' name all right ... like the Rainbow Trail out in Colorado an' the Grand Canyon which he had heard so much about an' never seen.

No wonder Luke Unwin and his gang were so intent on trailin' Dark Fury. It sure wasn't jest because of the hoss himself. No siree! They too, must be aware of what Lost Canyon contained, an' their only hope of finding it lay in keepin' close on the stallion's trail.

Kirk laughed quietly.

Them Cœur D'Alenes knew the secret of Lost Canyon all right, an' no doubt they would see to it that Luke Unwin and his pards did not get within a hundred miles of the place.

He relaxed then, humming to himself. A merry tune it was, all about the tumbleweeds and the secret places of the heart where was laughter all the long day through.

Clouds were racing high over the plain, trailing shadows along the uneven ground. Northwards, however, they were rolling low over scarcely discernible foothills, bringing in their wake a twilight that was almost that of evening.

Now and again there was a shimmering movement ahead of him where, like a miracle of green, long grass grew thick in some unexpected hollow – a green oasis in a world of rock; and the movement reminded him of invisible feet pressing eagerly on to some secret rendezvous ... another Lost Canyon mebbe.

Now that he knew that Dark Fury was definitely ahead of him, and not too far away at that, he was unusually light-hearted. No fear of pursuit from Luke Unwin troubled him. It would certainly take Unwin and his pals some little time to elude the Indians, by which time he might have a chance of reaching the Big Butte country.

Kirk suppressed the laugh that threatened to break the continuity of his song. Unwin and his men were not making such good progress after all. He even doubted that they would ever reach the boundaries of the Lost River Sinks although they might perhaps penetrate as far as the Big Butte country where he was to meet Washakie.

After that, Kirk felt that Washakie, with renewed forces at his command as he was sure to have, would see to it that Unwin did not proceed further into the forbidden land.

Meanwhile, as evening approached and Kirk drew nearer to the first scattering of hills, he saw the last of the blue sky become obscured with the increasing cloud masses, and the twilight that, all afternoon, had been visible well up the plain, was now deepening into a close resemblance of night. There was also clearly heard out on the trail a wailing coming from high up in the hills as a contrary wind went whistling through the many crevasses and gulleys.

It was in one of the small canyons that Kirk finally made ready to set up his camp for the night. As he set his horse free to graze upon a scant stretch of pasture he noticed heavy hoof marks that could belong only to one creature – the stallion he was trailing! The fact that they were still moist with the edges firm and unbroken showed clearly that they were as recent as the last hour or so.

Kirk therefore rested with greater confidence than ever that night, feeling sure that Dark Fury was not very far off.

The moaning of the wind, the fantastic race of clouds over the summits of the hills, was something altogether different from those similar incidents he had known in the border country farther south. They seemed so reminiscent of the mystery that existed out beyond the limits of the plain, and he, who had so often been alone in the silent watches of the night, and had experienced an aching void because of that loneliness, was now conscious that no more did the loneliness trouble him. By some strange chance, he was satisfied in the knowledge that there was something he greatly prized not too far off in the night. He was also aware of a curious affinity with the horse that had carried him in safety over all these miles.

Thus the whistle of the wind and interplay of cloud over the hills, while different from similar phenomena farther south, were yet part of the same pattern – a pattern that, whilst possessing a curious excitement, yet possessed a curious sense of peace.

When he finally fell asleep, no more was he aware of the rush of clouds over the hills and the moaning of the wind. He only knew that deep down in his heart was a soothing quietness, and it came from the far rooted knowledge that more than half the adventurous journey was over, and that he was at last in Idaho, and more than that, in the fabled Snake River Plain. Soon, very soon mebbe, there would be the Big Butte country, and after it, the Lost River Sinks and the Lost River Valleys. Finally ... and his mind was no longer retaining its hold on impressions ... finally, somewhere in the Lost River Range, was Lost Canyon itself ... Lost Canyon and Dark Fury ... Lost Canyon ... and Dark Fury....

The name of both canyon and horse seemed caught up in his throat ... caught and held there ... then gone ... gone in the breath of the sigh that brought him to a stranger canyon ... the canyon of dreamless sleep. ...

For the next week, Kirk continued to forge on ahead, always following that intricate trail blazed by Dark Fury. Where footprints were lacking to guide and encourage him, there was always some other sign to ensure him keeping to the right track.

He was not long in discovering that for most of the way, the entire plain seemed unchanging. Only the hills differed in shape and height, some little more than broken, wind-worn cliffs falling away into quite shallow canyons, others little more than a façade hiding a derelict expanse of boulder and scree.

On the eighth day of his long journey across the plain, Kirk noticed that the hills were assuming a less significant appearance. North of the main group seemed to lie a great corrugated territory that was entirely without shape or colour, and had the appearance of being as desolate as any desert in Utah.

Nevertheless, the farther he progressed along that inhospitable plain of rock and shallow basins, the more Kirk felt himself attracted to its austere grandeur, and more than once found himself wondering how he dare enter without a guide into this vast, up-flung fastness that was featureless and so utterly wild.

Yet, somewhere out in that world of rock was the one creature who had brought him thus far without mishap. Mebbe, the stallion was a better guide than any man, having perhaps a complete knowledge of the country that, farther north, seemed little better than world's end.

Kirk steeled himself to endure the loneliness and hardship he sensed existed for one such as he in that untrodden waste.

Day after day he rode the same featureless trail, sitting erect in the saddle, his eyes for ever peering ahead as if seeking to pierce the infinity of distance. The more he gazed to the north, the more did the ever remote horizon destroy his sense of proportion, finally taking away his sense of direction.

At last he was riding blindly onwards, not really knowing whether he was travelling north or north-west, for each mile was the same as the one that had preceded it, and each further mile as changeless as the countless others that had gone before.

Yet, despite the unchanging scene, there was the constant shouting of the wind which seemed to ebb and flow across the plain, and possessed not one voice, but many. In this alone, Kirk's judgement had not been at fault. He had known from the start that there would be strange sounds for ever assailing him in this northland wilderness where once a sea of molten lava bubbled and steamed.

Then late one afternoon, as he knelt to examine some recent horse droppings, thrilling to the knowledge that despite the sameness of the scene, he had yet kept hard on Dark Fury's heels, he noticed one other factor that brought a new interest into his speculations. There was now a thin layer of sand covering most of the rock, and in places, it was difficult to discern what was bare rock and what was a prolonged stretch of sand.

Kirk remounted his horse in a more thoughtful frame of mind, and as he forged on, with the sun westering on his left hand, he knew that before long he would come to the hills again, and perhaps to less inhospitable country.

His last night on the lava beds was the coldest he had yet encountered. In spite of the huge fire he had built up from some dry scrub he had found in what had once been another grassy hollow, he shivered as he slept wrapped in his blankets, and there were occasions when he heard his horse complaining, for the sand the animal had expected to find so much better to lie upon was still but a scant sprinkling over the rock.

Kirk was awake early, and was again on the trail as the sun came up, glowing redly.

Suddenly he pulled his horse to a halt. The plain was slipping away into a long slope, broken with stretches of green and in places marked with scrub-cedar. Beyond the green and the scrub-cedar, however, was the darker green of more luxuriant country, with the far-off shapes of ravines that clearly thrust up into hills which, from where he gazed, were lost in the haze of early morning.

The plain, none the less, was still to some extent subtly changing, until it ended in that deep green that appeared so pleasant to his eyes after the endless repetition of rock and the gloomy basins that all too often held water as black as the eye of night.

Then, scarcely a couple of hours after sun-up, he saw the first of the huge buttes – a huge, red uplift of rock that stood completely isolated where the green seemed to give way to what was either scrub or desert land.

As Kirk's eyes ranged backwards and forwards over that strange northern landscape, other outcrops became visible, some seeming like immense cattle standing petrified at the very gateway of the great northern mountains.

Kirk wasted very little time that day in resting and eating. He urged his horse on with all possible speed, and watched, as he came down out of the volcanic plain, how the outcrops became curiously magnified, growing from just mere mounds into enormous heaps.

By sundown, Kirk had reached another area of scrub-cedar, and as both he and his horse had travelled a great distance that day, both were in need of rest.

A protected spot was chosen as a camping site, and having set up his tent, Kirk stood gazing northwards. In the flaming of the afterglow from off some remote western hill, he witnessed the main butte taking on the appearance of a finely sculptured castle, complete with turrets and groined pillars, and knew that this was in actual fact the Middle Butte and that somewhere near it he was to meet Washakie.

What he did not know was that to reach it, he must first cross what was once the watercourse of Big Lost River – an area of greater barrenness than any he had encountered way back on the trail.

Kirk squared his shoulders as he gazed across the distance that separated him from the big butte country, and felt that the way to Lost Canyon was at last opening up.

Next day saw him drawing steadily nearer to Middle Butte, but when again at sunset he was forced to set up another camp, it seemed that the rocky outcrop was as far off as ever. The only indication he had that he was nearer to it by some miles was that the lesser buttes were taking on the appearance of immense hills.

Yet another day did he spend journeying across the vast plain, and by late afternoon, he glimpsed Big Southern Butte away off in what, to him, was the extreme west.

It was very tranquil that evening as he set up his camp, and kindled yet another fire out of the scrub he gathered with such care. Sound no longer had any significance in the scene. There was not the faintest suggestion of air, and the smoke from his fire rose upwards in one slow spiral.

After supper, he stood once again staring northwards. He found it difficult to withdraw his eyes from that northland horizon. The light that spilled across the plain from the west was limpid and of great strength. Both the buttes stood out in frowning boldness, Middle Butte seeming more than ever an immense sculptured castle, while the shape of Big Southern Butte was but a wall rising sheer on the horizon where the flaming fires of sunset flickered and played, and the limpid light flowed like water over all the plain.

Kirk felt that never had he known a sight so imposing as the sight of the two buttes rising out in the plain like landmarks erected by some ancient race of giants to guide travellers to the fabled land of the lost rivers.

He slept soundly again that night, and was away once more the moment the sun came up. He felt much refreshed and ready to travel for many hours without a break. His horse too, seemed energetic, and the moment Kirk set the animal on that lonely trail northwards, he stepped out with determination as if in eager response to his master's unspoken wishes.

By noon Kirk began to descend the great depression leading to what had been the watercourse of Big Lost River. The complete desolation of the ravine escaped his notice as he guided his horse onwards. So rapidly did he journey on that by late afternoon he was riding up out of the depression, having crossed the boulder-strewn river bed without mishap.

He gasped with amazement.

Not more than twenty miles away, Middle Butte soared with the dignity of a mountain out of the lava plain. If Sun Rock back in the Utah desert had possessed an awe-inspiring appearance, Kirk sensed that it must surely be dwarfed by comparison with Middle Butte here in Idaho. The entire formation rose in terraced steps – a groined mountain of surpassing beauty which now could be seen to have two distinct ridges with a deep ravine lying in between. Kirk guessed that the ravine was possibly the remnant of a volcanic crater.

A few miles farther out in the plain Kirk discerned what could only be Little Butte.

Thus, after many weeks of weary journeying, he had reached at last the Big Butte country that kept guard over the terrifying region of mountain and lake adjacent to the Lost River and Lemhi Ranges.

In the very act of patting his horse he realised suddenly that he was no longer alone. A horseman was on the trail ahead, riding more-over, towards him, and he knew at once that it was the Indian, Washakie.

Kirk rode down to meet him.

Chapter Twenty-two

For the next couple of days, Kirk was entertained by a small band of Cœur D'Alenes which had camped west of Middle Butte. The site chosen by the Indians was one that had been much used in the past, and, as far as Kirk could determine consisted of the only rich grazing in the locality. One red tepee had been set up in the centre of the camp. All around it were the packs and blankets of the band. While the Indians sat around and smoked endless pipes, only occasionally holding any conversation one with the other, their mustangs grazed contentedly, Kirk's own horse amongst them.

Kirk noticed that the mustangs were exceedingly graceful, certainly far removed from the usual 'bronco' he had hitherto encountered. They were also somewhat higher in the leg, and all, without exception, bore the stamp of good breeding.

It was not until he saw a pure black animal amongst them that Kirk realised that all had come from one blood-line, clearly that of Dark Fury.

He then understood only too well the truth of Washakie's statement back in Utah. The Cœur D'Alene horses were indeed a credit to the tribe, and undoubtedly an asset when it came to trading. Small wonder then that Washakie and the tribe were so greatly concerned to get Dark Fury back on that secret home range. It was not only Lost Canyon they wished to conserve, but the fine stock of animals that sprang from the stallion himself.

Although Washakie had greeted him warmly on their meeting way out in the plain, no word had as yet been said as to what the future held. Kirk had the impression that the whole band was waiting for something to happen, or some item of news to be conveyed to their Chieftain before broaching the subject of the stallion.

Save for the fact that Washakie had acknowledged Dark Fury's passage into the country beyond the buttes, nothing further was said.

On the third day, however, Kirk awakened to find the entire band astir. A rider had come in during the small hours of the morning with the news the Chieftain had been expecting.

Kirk was not kept long in ignorance as to its import.

Luke Unwin and his gang had succeeded in crossing the Snake River, and were already well north of Big Southern Butte, and pushing on towards the foothills of the Lost River Range.

Washakie approached Kirk gravely.

'Red Cloud, Cœur D'Alene Chieftain, bids me give message to white brother.'

The Indian paused for a moment, then put a slightly detaining hand on Kirk's shoulder.

'You done well. Make good journey an' keep close to wild hoss. Cœur D'Alenes much pleased.'

Taking his hand from Kirk's shoulder, Washakie moved back a pace without altering the steadfastness of his gaze.

'We go,' he said, 'to bring Cœur D'Alene vengeance on white men who disregarded warnin' given by tribe. They now must learn that to trail wild hoss without permission from tribe is dangerous.'

The Indian allowed himself the luxury of a smile before adding: 'You had permission because Red Cloud thinks you good for hoss. Now Red Cloud say you free to travel into Lost River country.'

There was another short pause as if Washakie was considering how best to impress upon his listener how great an honour had been bestowed upon him by Red Cloud. Then, almost abruptly Kirk thought, as if abandoning this line of thought and taking another which he considered more apt for the occasion, the Indian said:

'When next the moon is full over Valley of Little Lost, Cœur D'Alenes again meet white brother an' reward him as given in word of Washakie. Red Cloud now say you charged with takin' care of black stallion. When stallion joins up with wild hoss herd in Valley of Little Lost, you make camp an' wait Cœur D'Alene messenger. He bring you to tepee of Red Cloud. Cœur D'Alenes will see that stallion and herd return to Lost Canyon, an' wild hoss will never range Valley of Little Lost again.'

The Indian spoke slowly and distinctly, his last words being uttered with an air of finality as if a decision had already been made as to the stallion's future.

Kirk understood at last the reason for the three days' wait under the very shadow of Middle Butte. Had Unwin and his gang of desperadoes been thwarted in their efforts to regain the Big Butte country, he, Kirk, would never have been permitted to travel farther northwards. Now it was to be different. The entire band, under Washakie's leadership, was apparently to be used to rout Unwin and his friends. Kirk had very little doubt in his mind as to the outcome. This time it was extremely unlikely that the Indians would fail, and if they did, sooner or later, they would catch up with the gang. Until that moment, it seemed that he was to be the guardian of the stallion.

It suited Kirk very well indeed. Already he was within reach of his goal. The only puzzling feature about the whole affair lay concealed in Washakie's remark about the stallion being sent back into Lost Canyon and never more ranging the Valley of Little Lost. Just how the Indians proposed doing this was quite beyond his understanding. No doubt Lost Canyon itself would provide the answer.

There was a sudden flutter in his heart when he realised that such being the case, the faint hope he had cherished of perhaps one day making Dark Fury his own would never be possible. Even as he savoured the stab of disappointment, he knew deep down in his mind that he had never really thought that he would own the stallion. More correct perhaps would be to acknowledge the other secret hope ... to find Lost Canyon. That, at least, had never been a faint hope but a strong conviction so long as he kept close enough to the horse.

All this time Washakie had been watching him intently, and a little of what had been passing through Kirk's mind must have shown on his face, for the Indian shook his head in a disapproving manner.

'You travel to Valley of Little Lost with Cœur D'Alene's sanction which is good thing. To travel north without sanction, that is bad thing. Obey Cœur D'Alene's commands an' you be richly rewarded. There is much wealth where rainbow an' setting sun meet!'

He smiled enigmatically, then added: 'You go now an' collect stores for journey. We meet again when full moon rises over Valley of Little Lost. Farewell, white brother!' ·

The Indian turned sharply away and hurried to the red tepee where Kirk sensed Red Cloud himself was holding counsel with some of the others.

An hour later, the tepee had been dismantled and the tribe was departing north-west. Soon afterwards, with his wildly excited horse prancing around him, Kirk prepared the saddle packs and made ready to set out along the trail indicated to him by one of the band. He noticed that the track went straight between Middle and Little Butte, leading direct to the distant mountains and the Valley of Little Lost.

He knew that somewhere up that long valley, possibly shut in by the vast mountain masses of the Little Lost and Lemhi Ranges was the legendary Lost Canyon. The thrill he experienced at the knowledge was certainly heightened by the established fact that in the valley itself was a herd of wild horses, and that it was the very herd that Dark Fury had led until his capture by Luke Unwin.

As he rode along, thinking of all these things, Kirk felt that instead of waiting in the Valley of Little Lost for either Washakie or his messenger, he would do well if he remained close on Dark Fury's trail. He was sure that only by adopting such a measure could he ever hope to find Lost Canyon. It was clear that no member of the Cœur D'Alene tribe would permit him to make the journey once he had been contacted in the valley.

Thus as he travelled along the northland trail that morning, he was full of high hopes and a grim determination. As he passed close to the massive cliffs of Middle Butte he saw how the two ridges converged and slipped down towards a crater about which the retaining cliffs rose in one immense mass of stratified basalt.

In less than an hour, he entered into the locality of hidden caves and underground passages which was a favourite haunt of wild animals, including bear and deer.

Although he did not rest much that day, he still seemed a great distance from those hills and ravines he had glimpsed so many miles back. The only difference he could discern in them was that the peaks were no longer hidden from view, but were riding clear of the clouds, and the ravines wore a dusky aspect as if despite the bright day, they still retained the abandoned garments of night.

On the second day out from the Twin Buttes, Kirk encountered the first of the terrifying Sinks. It was no more than an enormous crater, with a winding runnel striking off north that, in some long forgotten hour of the world's history, had certainly been a river. He then saw that there were many similar runnels, and remembered having heard vaguely of the great gush of a Thousand Springs which pour in cascading torrents from the walls of Snake River Canyon many miles away in the south-west. The explanation, Kirk assumed, came from rivers that had been drained into Sinks such as the one he now saw, and continued to flow south-west to find an outlet through the innumerable gulleys of Snake River Canyon.

It was almost impossible to believe. Yet there could be no other explanation.

From that hour, Kirk rode on constantly pondering over this strange phenomena of the lost rivers. Thereafter, he kept his eyes on the alert, for there was much to see, and he was anxious to discover if the same tell-tale marks of lost watercourses terminated in the Sinks. It was not long before he confirmed his suspicions. Each sink had its runnels, and far down could be heard the faint sound of racing water, sweeping through some subterranean channel. Quite obviously many of the channels came from far north and carried water draining from rivers that rose way up in the mountains.

On the third day of his journey through the Sink country, the sun blazed hot above his head. As Kirk shaded his eyes the better to peer into the distance, he was pleased to notice at last that the mountains were so much nearer – range after range of them, all pine-clad up to the snow-line. He noticed also that the luxuriant green he had glimpsed so far back on the trail was no longer an illusion, but a definite indication of the great fertility of the country adjoining the immense mountain areas.

Moreover, Kirk began to discern other signs that roused him to excitement. The trail was now set over slightly gravelly ground, with here and there unmistakable signs of silt, and in the silt, clear impressions of hoof marks – not of just one animal, but many!

Kirk sensed he was approaching the meeting place of the wild horse herd mentioned by Washakie, and was confident that although he had seen no sight of Dark Fury for many days, the stallion was none the less in the immediate vicinity.

The barren nature of the country began to change rapidly. Whilst as yet there was no sage, there was at least a showing of soapweed and grass. Then without warning, so it seemed to Kirk, the whole plain ahead swelled upwards and broke against the foothills and the deeply recessed ravines. The mountain peaks were sharply defined on the skyline, the red rocks at the foot of the lesser hills giving colour to the scene.

At last the plain was no more. Kirk was about to enter into the region of mountain and lakes, following a trail that was now revealed as a smooth track striking up west of Saddle Mountain – a ten thousand foot peak on the Lemhi Range that contoured what was surely the bed of Little Lost River.

Kirk camped that night in the valley that was Dark Fury's ranging ground.

On that same day when Kirk Merrett passed up the trail west of Saddle Mountain, Dark Fury was penetrating well up the valley, and by late afternoon was within a mile or so of the place where the wild horses were peaceably grazing.

The stallion was in no great hurry to press on up the valley. He knew he was back in his old familiar surroundings. More than that, he sensed in the wind that the herd – his herd – was not far away.

A bear was moving up amidst a copse of juniper. Dark Fury watched the animal's progress with interest, disclosing no sign of alarm, only recognising in the huge, lumbering shape something that had always belonged to this land of mountain and canyon.

He whinnied approvingly, then glanced back along the trail to where the huge swell of cliffs buttressed the red-domed peak of Saddle Mountain. A drift of cloud was trailing gossamer-like across the ridge; northwards, another, more distant ridge, glowed in the crimson flare-path of the westering sun.

Then two very large-pinioned birds held his attention. They came gliding up the valley on a strong current of air, and Dark Fury knew them to be Grookah and Grannah – the two golden eagles who dwelt on an ancient eyrie set high up on Grouse Creek Mountain overlooking Lost Canyon.

Again the stallion whinnied, and closely watched the two birds as they flew in low, seeming to hover for a brief moment over the spot where he stood gazing upwards.

Suddenly he heard them bark one to the other, and the stallion knew that he had been recognised.

A second later they had gone – travelling the air-lines of the sky to Lost Canyon.

Dark Fury shook himself and heaved a long sigh. For the first time in many months, he was aware of a rare contentment. His long journey was practically at an end. There were no enemies in the Valley of Little Lost that he did not know and, if necessary, could not subdue.

Almost instinctively he sought out a scattering of larch and juniper encircling a shallow lake; and there, as dusk came encroaching up the valley, he stood relaxed until he felt the need for sleep. Lying down on the pine needles, he dozed, his nose set in a northerly direction so that it caught every trickle of air that came down to him from the ravine where the wild horses were.

When the cold clear light of the new day stood firmly in the Valley of Little Lost, Dark Fury moved on; and not far behind, came Kirk.

Never before had Kirk seen such a remarkable labyrinth of rock. Sage had put in an appearance on some of the nearby slopes, and brush and juniper straggled everywhere. The enormous rock formations marked the way from peak to peak, and all along the main ridges, so high above him, was the sharp gleam of frozen snow, with an occasional upheaval of red rock where the snow had melted away.

Then when he least expected it, he found himself travelling a downward course, and in less than an hour was approaching an amphitheatre that was vividly green, but completely hemmed in by bulging cliffs that zig-zagged up and up until they were lost to sight amidst the moving panorama of the sky.

Perhaps he was absolutely unprepared for what he saw next; perhaps he was still living in a dream-like state of wonder that when the whole significance of the sight burst upon him, he could only hold in his trembling horse and stare open-mouthed.

Less than half a mile away there was a wild milling of animals, all racing and screaming and scattering from north to south; and out-running them all was the black stallion that had once been a circus attraction back in Utah.

Dark Fury was rounding up his herd!

In moments, the entire band was hidden behind some monstrous rock formation; then the first of the mares would appear, running wild-eyed and with threshing hooves, closely pursued by some of the younger animals. Backwards and forwards the band went, first one way, then another; and always behind them, seeking to drive them into a closely-packed mass, was the snaking shape of the black stallion.

Tireless and determined, he continued his task, separating the young stallions from the mares. He seemd to be in all places at once – a black lightning flash that was relentless in its striking, that gave no respite and yet somehow was bringing order out of chaos and serenity out of turmoil.

At one stage of the proceedings, Dark Fury trumpeted like an enraged moose bull, and Kirk, concealed behind an overspill of boulders, felt his horse tremble violently at the sound. He patted the animal gently as if to reassure him, and then stared out across the arena in time to see Dark Fury driving in at another animal as black as himself. The mares packed themselves tightly together as if for protection and as if aware that Dark Fury was about to exercise his right to leadership, they froze into a stillness that brought complete silence to the amphitheatre.

In a matter of seconds, the two black horses stood facing each other, less than twenty paces apart.

Once again Dark Fury uttered that queer trumpeting cry, and snaking forward, reared up and brought his fore-feet crashing down upon his enemy. Dark Fury's attack was made with a suddenness that took the other horse by surprise. The next moment, however, both stallions were whirling and striking at each other, Dark Fury gaining an advantage by suddenly locking his forelegs around the other's neck.

Both beasts staggered like wrestlers; until the younger horse broke away, and with ears closely pressed against his skull, fled northwards, leaving Dark Fury the victor.

In that moment of achievement, the stallion uttered no cry of triumph. He stood like a statue at the head of the amphitheatre, surveying the herd.

Kirk watching him, knew then that whether or not he found Lost Canyon, what he had just witnessed had made the long journey he had undertaken more than worthwhile. He had seen the real Dark Fury in action, and it was the experience of a lifetime!

Chapter Twenty-three

All was quiet in the Valley of the Little Lost River for the rest of that day. The herd did not attempt any breakaway, most of the animals having recognised Dark Fury as their old leader.

Following the hasty departure of the over-impetuous horse that had challenged Dark Fury's right to assume control after so long an absence, most of the mares had gone back to their grazing. Even the young yearling stallions which Dark Fury had segregated from the main herd, had accepted the position. Many of them when still inexperienced colts had been brought down from Lost Canyon for the spring grazing in the Valley of Little Lost, and they had vivid memories of the stallion's exploits during the trek. The huge black horse was, as well they knew, an exceedingly hard taskmaster when the occasion demanded it of him.

As for Kirk, no more beautiful day could he remember having spent in such ideal surroundings. The few clouds that passed high over the Valley of Little Lost sent an ever-changing pattern of sunlight and shadow sweeping from one end of the glen to the other. Blue-birds continually called way up in the junipers, and a lone mocking bird kept up a shrill whistle from the copse beside the shallow lake where Dark Fury had slept the night.

Twice that afternoon the two eagles Grookah and Grannah from Grouse Creek Mountain came sailing leisurely overhead, and each time Dark Fury marked their passage with a steady eye. It was not until the sun began to go down behind the Little Lost Range and the shadows started to drop quickly over the valley that Dark Fury made his last patrol of the day. He went at an even trot around the amphitheatre, pausing only at the southern end when he discerned the smoke from Kirk's camp fire rising upwards.

Now, more than ever did Dark Fury accept Kirk Merrett's presence as something closely allied to his own existence; and so, satisfied that all was well with the herd, the stallion took up a position on a low ridge the better to gaze down upon the valley and watch the spiral of smoke with peaceful eyes.

Even as it had been a truly lovely day, so too was it a lovely night. The first star shone direct over the distant northern peak which the stallion would have readily recognised as Grouse Creek Mountain. Soon, in the paling evening sky, there appeared other stars, all twinkling like lamps lit way up in the airlines of the sky which only the eagles knew ... and low down, where the red dome of Saddle Mountain was but a dark smudge on the horizon, came the slow uplifting of a silver boat ... the new moon!

Kirk beheld the rising of the ship of night, and a sudden catch in his heart reminded him of Washakie's words ... 'We meet again when full moon rises over Valley of Little Lost ....'

As he lay on his back, with his hands clasped under his head, he pondered carefully over the Indian's words. Washakie had known that when once the stallion joined up with the herd, he would probably remain in the valley for many days ... possibly much longer than the sixteen days that must pass before the moon was at the full.

The more he considered the matter, the more did he realise how frail now was his chance of ever discovering Lost Canyon. Without the aid of Dark Fury to lead him to it, he knew he could never find it.

But, as sleep came stealing over him and the silver ship of the moon rose high over Saddle Mountain, his mind relinquished its hold on the hope of visiting Lost Canyon, and he only knew that the night breeze was cool on his cheeks, and that a long way up the valley, a night bird was calling, sharp and clear, but tenderly musical.

Perhaps he fell asleep dreaming of the night bird's song, and the soaring ship of the moon; perhaps it was all a dream too – that rocky mountain he thought he could see so clearly ... and the deep valley that lay beyond. Maybe too, no more than a dream the pine tree as big as any pine could be ... and a waterfall that fell tossing from off a mountain ledge ... and a rainbow that fell in an arc of loveliness towards the sunset.

All dreams, maybe; but certainly no dream that distant clamour breaking in upon his subconscious meanderings ... a clamour of hooves beating a tattoo away off in the fastnesses of the valley, and a high, sustained trumpeting like a bugle note winding up to bid him awake and follow.

Kirk awoke and saw no more the moon high over Saddle Mountain, and heard no more the night bird's song. All he could see was the morning sky with the last stars fading, and heard, hard and sharp in his ears, the steady echoes of feet tramping away from him ... a hundred, hundred feet, and one last call floating up to him ... the call of a stallion who had set out in the golden light of dawn to trek to Lost Canyon!

Ten minutes later, he had broken camp, and was riding quickly down the valley, following that distant line of horses that moved slowly between the towering walls of the mountains to that immense peak that rose many miles to the north ... Grouse Creek Mountain!

A warm wind came blowing from off the very high hills. Way over against Borah Peak on the Little Lost River Range, was a flight of wild geese. Soon their honking echoed down the valley. For a moment or two, the sunlight quivered with their passing, then a stillness closely akin to austerity possessed the whole glen from north to south. Not a sound disturbed the quietness. It was almost uncanny. There was not even an echo ringing out from the hooves of the many moving feet as the wild horse herd, driven by Dark Fury, went steadily up along the fertile river basin, slowly approaching an even greater frown of mountains which, in their soaring, seemed to shut out the sky.

All that bright day, and the next, the great trek continued, with Kirk Merrett, full of wonder at what was taking place, following as close as he dare on the very heels of the magnificent black stallion.

About the middle of the afternoon on the third day, the band of horses began to ascend a clearly refined gulley that struck upwards north-west of a narrow lake like a finger pointing the way to some hidden break in the mountain chain.

Kirk's heart beat high with hope. This surely was the trail that led direct to Lost Canyon. He could see it mounting higher and higher above the blink of the little lake, ascending very steeply indeed at one point until, like a piece of string, frayed out and done, it disappeared into what seemed a fissure in the mountain wall.

Yet there was something decidedly odd about that track. It was so deeply scored in the hillside, and in places full of débris and boulders. There were also great hollows in it, some as much as three feet in depth.

At last Kirk understood. He was travelling what had once been a river bed, possibly that of the Little Lost River itself.

His excitement grew.

Throughout the whole of that afternoon and well into the slow gathering evening the trek went on, and then as the silver slip of the moon began to rise once again over the now far distant dome of Saddle Mountain, Kirk discovered that the herd ahead of him was no longer on the move but grazing on a small plateau between the up-rising walls of the mountain.

He was hard put to find a suitable place to set up his camp in such a desolate neighbourhood. Although he had not been aware of the fact, the boulder-strewn trail had ascended farther up the slope than he had thought possible, and he was not too far from what, way down, had been the frayed end of the track. Nevertheless, he managed to discover an ancient cedar, dwarfed and very old, set high up on a bank, and close to it, a patch of grass suitable for his horse.

Soon he was snugly wrapped in his blankets, and the sight of the towering hills now steeped in darkness brought a sharp stab of dread to his mind. Supposing in the night the band of horses returned and stampeded at sight of him? What then would be the end for both himself and the horse who had carried him so faithfully all these past weeks?

As if in answer to his strange forebodings, up amidst the hidden peaks the wind moaned and cried loudly in the cedars that clung to them with the desperation of living things whose day was nigh over and who so soon would be tossed into eternity.

Kirk snuggled deeper into his blankets. He could hear the munching of his horse. Then, a while later, the far-off barking of a hill-fox. After that, nothing, for sleep came, deep and profound until at daybreak he was awakened by the cold.

Sunrise from this high spot above the valley was a thing of incredible beauty. Far down the trail, the slope slipped away towards that narrow finger of the lake, and stretching out beyond it, the entire scene was a widening basin fringed here and there with cedars and junipers, with the surrounding hills breaking into small creeks and canyons. At the very head of the valley, Saddle Mountain dominated the scene, snow-clad above the skyline, with only the red dome of its summit glinting in the morning light. Then the outline of the mountain became more clearly seen, the snow on the ridge holding the yellow of gold poured in a running stream from some giant cauldron in the sky.

Not long afterwards, Kirk was once more in the saddle, and following again that slow-moving herd of horses that, an hour before, had started on the last stage of the trek to Lost Canyon.

The day seemed endless, each mile of the upward thrusting trail becoming interminable as the gorge narrowed. Only once that day did he get a glimpse of Dark Fury, now quite three miles ahead of him. Not many minutes later as the sun glowed redly above the western line of hills, he realised that he could no longer see the stallion, or the herd. The frowning mountains had taken them as surely as if they had never been.

From that hour, Kirk guessed that his journey to Lost Canyon would be by the means of following the herd's spoors as best he could.

Kirk spent a very restless night, once again painfully aware of the cold at such a high altitude. He was only too glad to kindle an early fire and prepare a hot meal. Then, as on the previous day, the sun was scarcely above the horizon when he again set off up the trail, entering now a shallow depression flanked high up on either side by dwarf cedars. He noticed that the farther he travelled along the ever-narrowing gorge, the gloomier it became. Then he found himself approaching what was an enormous cavern set in the wall of the mountain, and the trail vanished into it, filling Kirk with a measure of uncertainty as to its ultimate destination.

Nevertheless, it was obvious that the band of wild horses driven by Dark Fury, had gone through into the darkness to some predestined point.

Dismounting to examine the débris-covered track the more thoroughly, he got a shock when he discovered close against the cavern wall a cask of the type used to transport gunpowder.

Kirk was not long in finding that the cask did indeed contain explosive powder, sufficient, he calculated, to cause a considerable landslide.

His next thought brought a wave of excitement. Perhaps the tunnel led to Lost Canyon, and the stories he had heard about the wealth it contained were not only true, but others also knew the Canyon's secret, and were intent on mining the area. There could be no other explanation for the presence of the powder cask.

In addition, he discovered some specially prepared brushwood bundles, clearly intended to be used as torches. This lent support to the idea that mining activities were contemplated by somebody or other.

Taking as many of the bundles as could be conveniently placed in the saddle packs, he lit one for his immediate use, and holding it aloft, grasped his horse by the bridle and started the laborious journey through the cavern. The very instant he entered the darkness, he experienced a strong current of air blowing through from some distant opening.

He felt encouraged, and his heart beat high. The lighted brand disclosed that the tunnel retained an even height, and that the floor was composed of small pebbles with here and there a clear run of sand. More strongly than ever was the fact impressed upon him that he was traversing an ancient river course.

It was a little after high noon when he entered the cavern. At times, the cold stream of air was sharp against his face, so sharp in fact that he was forced to close his eyes and gasp for breath.

After a while, the floor became more sandy than otherwise, and his footfalls and those of his horse were completely silenced. Kirk could see, however from the fitful glow of the torch, that the sand was broken and churned as if by countless feet having passed over it, and he knew that the feet had been the hooves of the band of wild horses, and their leader, Dark Fury.

Suddenly his horse tugged against the bridle, forcing Kirk to come to a halt. He heard the animal whistling through his nostrils with fear. Glancing down, he gave a gasp of horror. A few feet away was a deep crevasse in the floor of the cavern. Cold sweat trickled down his forehead. But for his horse and the uncanny sense animals have of approaching danger, he might have plunged headlong into it, for it was in the very centre of the track.

He noticed that the left-hand wall of the cavern thrust away a little from the crevasse, and judging from some firmly made hoof marks, the wild horses had passed the spot in single file, and quite clearly without mishap for there was no sign of violently disturbed sand or gravel.

Kirk summoned up all his reserves of courage. Stroking his horse gently and speaking reassuringly to him, he proceeded forward with care, keeping close to that widening bulge in the wall, and making doubly sure that the animal was well on the inside and as far from the crevasse as was possible.

In a couple of minutes the danger spot was passed, and pausing, Kirk peered into that awesome break in the tunnel floor. He kindled another torch of brushwood casting the remains of the old one into the gap.

It fell out of sight, the flame flickering then suddenly sweeping up before guttering into nothingness. In that brief flickering, however, Kirk had seen enough. He had glimpsed the fissure disappearing into a void that was too terrifying to contemplate. He wondered no longer why rivers seemed to be forever disappearing in this strange country. Before him was a plain answer. The crevasse was yet another sink.

The air was cleaner as he advanced, with a fragrance in it. That was it! A fragrance such as one might find in a breeze blowing from off a lofty mountain range covered with larch and pine. Then Kirk knew! Rosin! That was the fragrance. Rosin!

He hurried on, his excitement rising and his heart beating wildly. He was so engrossed in moving steadily into the wind that he failed to notice another tunnel branching off from the right. Even had he seen it, he would not have considered following it, for the hoof prints still lay thick in the trail at his feet.

Despite the darkness and the limitations imposed on his vision by the feeble glow of the torch, he had lost his sense of fear. He knew that he was following what had once been a watercourse whose age was perhaps a million years or more. He knew too that the horrifying darkness was as impenetrable as any he had ever known, and that the silence, save for the fall of his feet and those of the horse in the soft sand, was a silence fraught with danger. But Dark Fury and his herd of wild horses had passed this way, and the end of the grim underground trail could not be too far off. The wind told him that. The wind . . . .

As it increased in force, a sudden surge of panic rose to match it. Fear clutched at his heart. He thought chaotically: Now I am in the very bowels of the earth . . . under a mountain. There might be other crevasses. There might be the sudden rising of a river. . . .

He heard a voice – his own voice strangely distorted, saying: 'Take care! Have a grip on yourself. Dark Fury and the herd came this way. It's the way to Lost Canyon . . . Lost Canyon . . . .'

He found himself laughing mirthlessly, then was aware of tears dimming his eyes and his tongue cleaving heavy and thick to his mouth.

The grip on his heart tightened, and silence and solitude were no more, for reaching out to him from some place not far off came an ominous sound, the muffled roar of falling water . . . .

He paused in his tracks, gasping, but his horse nudged him on; the beast was wiser than he. There was no danger for him in that distant roar of water. More important, the horse could sniff not only the scent of rosin, but grass also – rich grass, and he was impatient to reach it.

The rush of wind against Kirk's face was colder and stronger than ever. The roar of the water was a part of it. Another wave of fear swept over him, turning into absolute panic as the torch flickered, the flame suddenly rising and throwing distorted shadows on the walls of the cavern. He glimpsed for a fleeting second the roof above him from which stalactites, like tusks, gleamed ominously then were lost in darkness as the torch guttered and went out.

From a moment of seeing to a moment of blindness was eternity in that terrible underworld of wind and sound. He stumbled forward, and suddenly the darkness was not the same darkness; light filtered through from some place ahead – grey light. As Kirk moved forward, it changed to golden. A minute ... two perhaps ... three ... even four ... he did not know. He couldn't tell. All he knew was that the opening came steadily nearer, and framed against it, a silvery fall that was water tumbling from a great height; and beyond the water and the gold, mountains and trees ... and way up, beyond both ... the sky ... a blue sky ... a very blue sky ....

'Oh, thank God! Thank God!' and while the words still echoed like a prayer in his mind, he found himself standing on a grassy plateau close to the spumy fall of water. Then with eyes dazed with wonder, he gazed down at long last upon Lost Canyon – the last remaining sanctuary of the wild horse herds and the many wild animals who sought to live in peace away from man – the destroyer of their kind!

Chapter Twenty-four

Not at any time during the hazardous trek through the tunnel had Kirk been absolutely sure of what he would find at the other end. Indeed, during the last few yards, he had no clear thoughts on the matter at all, being conscious only of the terrible dread that had followed on the heels of the fear that had gripped him at the distant sound of the cascading water. Thus, on reaching the grassy plateau, he could only stand, dazed with wonder, trying to take in the whole scene that lay before him.

The greatest contrast was in the bright light that poured down from an exceedingly blue sky. It was dazzling in its intensity after the awesome darkness of the underground passage through the mountain. The next contrast was in the extraordinary nature of the rock formation. For the most part, the cliffs were bright red below the snowline, although some of the higher hills were well timbered and were steel-grey in colouring as they soared eight thousand feet or more above the floor of the valley.

Perhaps the most startling of the cliff structures were in the immediate vicinity of the plateau. The towering walls of bright rock ascended into beautifully sculptured turrets, with here and there an occasional pinnacle, emblazoned after the manner of an obelisk. One such obelisk apparently split a run of water a thousand feet or so above the plateau, causing two distinct falls to cascade down into the valley to form a lake of quite considerable proportions.

As far as Kirk could see, the entire valley was some fifteen miles in extent, running obliquely from north-west to south, and being perhaps a little more than five miles in depth.

It could only be one place – the place he had heard so much about and had longed so ardently to reach – Lost Canyon! He had reached his journey's end; and for Dark Fury and his band of wild horses bunched north of the lake, it was journey's end too.

As he led his horse slowly down the well-marked track that more or less followed the run of water from the cliff above, Kirk noticed that he was approaching what could only be described as the broken walls of a magnificent mountain paradise. The ruins, however, were not in the same state of decay that had characterised the contours of Sun Rock way back in Utah. In fact, these ruins were likely to last as long as time itself, for the rock, despite its bright colouring, was yet hard at the core, and clearly of volcanic origin.

It took Kirk the best part of an hour to reach the floor of the valley, and glancing up, he saw that the sun was well down the western sky.

He searched around for a camping site. It was then he discerned the most important sign of all necessary to convince him that he was in Lost Canyon. As he glanced back at the fall of water, he saw what at first seemed another rainbow bridge, similar to the one in the canyon bordering the Utah desert. This bridge, however, was of a less tangible nature, being little more than a delicate ensemble of colours, quivering like a slender arc across the entire valley.

Washakie's words again rang loud and clear in his ears . . . 'There is much wealth where rainbow an' settin' sun meet . . . .'

Kirk unconsciously turned his gaze westwards and glimpsed what was a river, with the rainbow seeming to dip right into it.

Before he could take in any more details, the light faded from the western cliffs and a purple darkness stood where the river had been. Then, beating their way across the glen were two shapes who, on reaching what was apparently a favourable current of air, suddenly glided effortlessly to their eyrie on Grouse Creek Mountain.

They were Grookah and Grannah, the golden eagles.

Swiftly then, the shadows dropped down across the entire valley, and the rainbow bridge was no more. Not many minutes afterwards, the moon, now well in its first quarter, came soaring up behind the eastern hills, and so began Kirk's first night in Lost Canyon.

Early next morning, Kirk was up and about, intending to make a careful examination of the canyon. Before doing so, he searched for a more permanent camping place, and chose a site under what appeared to be the largest pine he had ever seen.

Maybe there was a vague probing of frail fingers in his mind as he re-erected his tent. Whatever it was, he failed to understand why he should have the feeling that he had set up his tent under a similar tree before. He had forgotten the dream of a few days before when he seemed to glimpse a valley similar to the one in which he now found himself, and with it a tree as tall as this pine under which he had now erected his tent.

Perhaps he was over-anxious to explore the canyon and therefore did not delve too closely into the strange familiarity that existed in his mind. He worked quickly and methodically, and was soon ready to be away on his journey of exploration.

Dark Fury watched him ride up past the lake, and as the herd moved restlessly at the approach of one alien to the valley, the stallion stood in readiness to head off any aggressive move his charges might make.

Kirk, in Lost Canyon, was now his responsibility!

The young fellow spent the whole day riding along the fantastic trails that seemed to lie at the base of every mountain. There was so much to be seen and so more to marvel at. He realised that there must be every known type of wild life gathered in the canyon, ranging from mule deer, elk and antelope to mountain sheep and goats, with a goodly number of bears. There was moreover the distinct possibility that somewhere up on the higher slopes roamed a mountain lion or two, although not a single one did he see on his excursion.

Of bird life, apart from the golden eagles, there were bald eagles, ravens, blue-birds, and most of the other birds native to the north-western territories of the Rockies.

Among the varying belts of timber, Kirk noticed some fine Douglas Fir, a quantity of Englemann Spruce and Lodgepole Pine.

He returned to his camp satisfied and intrigued with all that he had seen, confident that Lost Canyon was the one remaining paradise for all animals of the wild, and the greatest of these was Dark Fury, who had moved in closer to the camp during his absence. Nor did the stallion move far away when Kirk finally set his horse free to graze while he prepared his evening meal.

It was another wonderful night, with the moon soaring high over the valley and the twin falls toppling like cascades from the rocky heights hidden in the night.

Perhaps Kirk slept late the next morning; perhaps he had already lost all sense of time in the canyon, but when he eventually awoke, it was quite three hours after sun-up.

The herd of wild horses had moved far up the valley, but Dark Fury was no more than a couple of hundred yards away.

Watching the stallion, Kirk began to have once again constant urgings to try and possess the horse for his own. The stallion clearly trusted him; would he object to the control of a halter, he wondered.

As the day went on, he abandoned his original idea of visiting the river in the western part of the valley. Instead, he fostered the thought of capturing Dark Fury. He recalled that first meeting with the stallion in Burke's corral where the animal was held prisoner. He remembered too, the strong impression he had gained – that the horse before him was an animal that could never be run off his feet, but one who would hold his own with the best of them, and carry his rider over the sage with a sureness of movement that would be like floating on a cloud . . . .

That night he slept little, and it seemed that the dawn would never come so that he could gaze upon the stallion once again, and renew once more the game of make-believe that might, even now, cease to be a game but a reality. His desire to possess the stallion had become an obsession.

His dreaming was rudely brought to an end in the one reality he did not expect in Lost Canyon. A little after daybreak there came a wild screaming out by the lake, and in the dim light of morning, Kirk could see Dark Fury racing like a black thunderbolt around the herd as if bent on marshalling some of the horses into a mobile semi-circle.

As he ran in the direction of his own animal who was standing startled by the unexpected round-up, he saw with dismay the reason for Dark Fury's anger.

Luke Unwin and his gang had invaded Lost Canyon!

The four men were within half-a-mile of the herd, and obviously bent in separating Dark Fury from the protection of the other horses and recapturing him.

Kirk hastily saddled his horse and prepared to move into the arena, determined to do all he could to save the stallion from another fate possibly worse than the one from which he had escaped.

Dark Fury, with native cunning, had formed some twenty of the younger animals into a half-circle. Screaming again with rage, he took the lead, and with tossing mane and racing hooves, drove out towards the horse thieves with his selected part of the herd thundering behind him.

No man could hope to withstand such an onslaught as Dark Fury contemplated making on Luke Unwin and his friends. Clearly, the stallion intended destroying the men remorselessly.

Unwin and the others realised this, and swinging around, went racing back towards the lake and the narrow trail that wound up to the plateau and the tunnel in the mountain side.

All Kirk could do was sit and watch. The sudden attack of the wild horses held him spellbound with fear and amazement.

As he witnessed the grim event, the day grew in splendour over the hills, and an almost liquid radiance spilled down into the valley that was Lost Canyon.

The stallion's mad rush towards his enemies had roused in his followers a fury that nigh outmatched his own. Even when the four men started up the ascent to the plateau, Dark Fury did not slacken in his pursuit. He simply swung away from the lead, and racing around the flank of the herd, took up a position in the rear which drove the horses up the trail behind the fleeing men.

Thirty minutes or more went by; the sun was well up above the mountains when Kirk beheld the last of the horses – possibly Dark Fury himself – disappearing from sight on the plateau. With a shock he realised that the wild horses were continuing the pursuit through the tunnel.

He knew then as surely as he knew that within a few days the moon would rise full over the Valley of Little Lost, that Unwin and his friends were doomed. No more would they persecute Dark Fury. What the Cœur D'Alenes had failed to do, the stallion, with the herd at his side, would accomplish.

It was hopeless to think of following, for he could imagine nothing worse than to be trapped under the mountain by the herd unexpectedly returning. In the darkness of the underground trail they would trample him to death.

The only course left open to him was to explore the canyon still further and await the return of Dark Fury.

He therefore rode slowly over to the lake with a view to exploring the region of the falls. By mid-day, he had made an important discovery. The falls came from a tarn set high up in the groin of the mountain. An examination of the tarn itself resulted in yet another discovery. It was fed by a series of springs which, at some period long past, had carved out a deep watercourse that ended in the inevitable sink.

The most puzzling feature of all about the falls was the way in which they had been formed. A huge pinnacle, crashing from the nearby cliffs, had diverted the main flow of water, with the result that the lesser overspill cascaded down in the direction of the plateau and the tunnel, while the larger torrent fell in a curtain of spray direct into the lake.

Kirk felt that Lost Canyon must be made up of many such miracles of rock formation. One further discovery he made. Proceeding up beyond the tarn, he came to what appeared to be the only divide in the chain of mountains that enclosed Lost Canyon. On reaching it, he found it to be an immense precipice with a drop of some four thousand feet on the eastern slope. From it, however, he could gaze down upon the panorama of the Valley of Little Lost, even to the extent of discerning the tortuous trail by which he had ascended to the ramparts of the mountain group enclosing the hidden canyon. Of Dark Fury and the herd, not a sign could he see. The entire outer valley was but a checkered pattern of grey and green, brought alive by the racing of clouds and sunshine over the floor of the glen and the opposing mountain slopes.

Late in the afternoon, when Kirk was again down by the lake, he began to have misgivings about the weather. A bank of cloud had crept up above the western skyline.

Within an hour he knew that a storm was inevitable. A wave of wind, accompanied by a ripple of light, crossed the valley from the west. Then he heard a distant roar which, caught up in the mountains, came pealing down in heavy echoes.

The remnant of the wild horse herd had disappeared. Both young stallions and mares were sheltering in a narrow accilvity. They had experienced many such storms in the past, and were anxious to get what cover they could from the relentless rain when it finally came.

All too soon came the full impetus of the storm, breaking with violence behind the vast piling of clouds. There was a wild crying in the trees, and Kirk and his horse, both sheltering in a break in the nearest cliff, heard the sound as something reaching out from the storm to engulf them.

For an hour, the lightning flashed from peak to peak, and when the rain came, it was a cloudburst that almost obscured the entire valley in its cloak of grey.

Kirk was not quite sure whether it was thunder that brought a tremor to the earth beneath his feet, or whether a fall of rock was responsible. He only knew that both he and the horse stood closer together until the rain ceased and they were able to leave their temporary refuge which was fast becoming a new watercourse.

Kirk had not gone more than a few yards before he was brought to a sharp halt. His eyes opened wide with wonder as he gazed at the twin falls in spate. The full flow of water was a writhing curtain of foam that billowed outwards and drifted away in a skein of mist before swelling the already turbulent undercurrents of the lake. Then he saw with dismay what the floating mist almost concealed. Part of the cliff above the tunnel had collapsed, and from the wide scattering of débris, Kirk knew that the only entrance to the outside world was closed for ever.

All that was left was the gulley-like trail, twisting up and up to the divide that was but a ridge overlooking the Valley of Little Lost.

What conflicting fears he experienced at the discovery were suddenly thrust from him by the gradual formation of the rainbow, bridging the valley from east to west. The storm clouds were passing over, and the sun was going down in a sepia-tinted sky behind the western peaks.

Whether or not he would ever leave the canyon again was of little importance compared to that other thought that came to him in an overpowering surge. He could not resist searching for what might be at the end of the rainbow.

He hastily mounted his horse, and with a wild shout, sent the bewildered animal racing madly across the canyon, his mind echoing again those words of Washakie's ... 'There is much wealth where rainbow an' settin' sun meet....'

The rainbow was fading rapidly when Kirk finally reached the river which was swollen with flood water. He flung himself out of the saddle. Falling on his stomach, he gazed down into a deep pool, and his eyes beheld the truth of the Indian's words. A dull gleam came up at him from the depths ... the gleam of sand, the colour of gold ....

Then Kirk knew! He uttered a wild cry of excitement. It *was* gold. Not only the pool, but the whole of the river bed was a mass of gold washings!

Gold! Untold wealth ... and at the end of the rainbow just as Washakie had foretold.

Suddenly Kirk buried his head in his hands to stem the tears of disappointment that began to dim his vision. Of what use the gold to him now? There was little hope of him ever gaining the outside world again. More than that, more than any wealth, he wanted Dark Fury – the greatest of great stallions.

He rode back across the canyon to the place where his tent stood under the tallest pine he had ever seen, and the moon, a yellow half-moon, began to climb up the sky, flooding the whole valley with a new kind of gold as if to match that which lay deep in the pools of that western river.

Kirk understood at last why Unwin and his men had invaded the canyon. It was not only for Dark Fury they had risked their lives and travelled so far. They too knew of the gold the river contained, were maybe responsible for the cask of gun powder concealed at the entrance to the tunnel.

For most of that night, Kirk lay unsleeping, tormented by the knowledge of the gold in the river. The thought of it pursued him down the unending corridors of restless dreaming that lay halfway between sleeping and waking, and all the while the yellow half-moon continued to soar over the valley.

It was a long, a very long night.

Epilogue

Sleep came to him an hour or so before dawn, and then only to bring him further dreams of the canyon – the last refuge of wild life; but no longer was he tormented with the desire for gold.

He opened his eyes wearily, conscious of the sun shining down upon him, and after a few moments, he rolled over on to his side.

As a sharp whinney came from his horse, he raised himself on to his elbow. The animal was staring in the direction of the twin falls.

From behind the spread of the largest of the overspills came a number of horses – the very horses Dark Fury had led in the stampede to drive his enemies from the canyon.

Kirk stared in amazement, conscious of a sudden upsurge of joy in his heart, when he saw the stallion himself move slowly from under the veil of water. Dark Fury paused for a moment knee deep in the lake before scrambling up on to the rocky shore. Fifteen minutes later, the young stallions had rejoined the main herd, and their leader was standing like a sentinel watching over them.

That day was the grandest and most important in the whole life of Kirk Merrett. A brief examination of the lake and the waterfall disclosed another tunnel, the entrance to which was completely hidden by the immense run of water from off the cliff. He remembered then Dark Fury's fondness for standing under a fall of water in that other canyon in Utah. Now he understood why and his heart sang with gratitude to the great black stallion who had revealed to him the secret of the lake.

As the day wore on, Kirk became conscious of a strange inner peace which pervaded his whole being. He saw Dark Fury as a king reigning supreme over his subjects, and he saw too, that he, mere man, had no right to seek to bend such a king to his own will. Slowly, the desire to possess the stallion faded from his mind, and with it, too, went his lust for the gold.

To return to the outer world in possession of so much wealth would never escape unnoticed. Other men, greedy as he had once been for riches, would penetrate into the Lost Canyon. They would pillage and destroy, and it would mean the end of Dark Fury's kingdom, and the end of the peace for every wild thing there.

Thus, his greatest moment came when he resolved to leave the canyon by the new route Dark Fury had shown him, and to preserve forever the secret of the Canyon. He decided to leave the very next day.

It was a fine morning he chose for his departure. Not a sign of the recent storm remained. The weather was obviously settled. The sky was again the dazzling blue that was a blue beyond describing. Even the few wispy clouds of the previous evening had gone. The breeze coming down from off the mountains was the merest trickle, veering from north to north-west.

As he finished the last meal he was to have in the canyon, he was surprised to find Dark Fury approaching slowly from the direction of the lake. It was as though some strange intuition, acutely developed in animals who dwelt in a wild state, was warning the stallion that Kirk was about to take leave of him and the canyon.

Very slowly indeed did Dark Fury come in close to the camp under the pine, to remain but a few yards distant while the young man took down the tent and started to stow away his belongings in the saddle packs.

Then as Kirk stamped out the remains of the fire, the stallion moved in even closer, and whinnied softly.

Kirk straightened his back, and still in a squatting position, looked up at the horse. A sigh escaped his lips. Never before had the stallion seemed so graceful a creature, and possessed of such gentleness. All fierceness had gone from him, and in his eyes glowed the soft light of understanding. It was as if Dark Fury knew that never again would he see Kirk Merrett who, way back in Utah, had befriended him and had saved him from an ignoble end in the red swamp of the desert.

The stallion whinnied again and then pawed the ground gently while he lowered his head.

Kirk rose to his feet, and crossing quietly towards the horse did what he had wanted to do from the very first day he set eyes on him. Without fear, he stretched out his hand and rubbed the sleek nose. The stallion seemed to quiver with delight.

For a short moment of time Kirk gazed into the dark, almost slumberous eyes of the great horse, realising that truly he no longer wanted to make the animal his own.

As he stood there, close to the stallion, he resolved to seal off the canyon, and make it eternally safe for those who dwelt in it. This was a debt of honour he owned his regal friend.

Dark Fury, moving back a pace, indicated to Kirk with a shake of his head that the brief moment of intimacy between them was at an end. Sadly, yet with a strange surge of expectancy in his heart for what he was to do, Kirk moved towards his own horse.

Sitting half-crouched, with the reins held loosely in his hands, he looked once more upon Dark Fury. The words choked in his throat. 'Goodbye, big feller ... goodbye .... '

Then because he could think of nothing further to add, he probed his mount into movement, and rode swiftly away from the tallest pine he had ever seen and the finest stallion he had ever known.

Dark Fury made no attempt to follow. He understood that the one man to whom he might have surrendered his heart had made the decision for him, and that he was to remain behind in Lost Canyon, to keep for ever that freedom which was his heritage and the heritage of those who would follow as a result of his leadership of the wild horse band.

Only when he witnessed Kirk riding into the lake did he make a sudden move to follow. Then he seemed to dig himself in, his hind hooves set in the warm ash of the fire that Kirk had stamped out.

Then as Kirk, with a further glance back, drove his horse behind the curtains of the fall, Dark Fury raised his head and sent winding after him one last trumpeting call of farewell.

The sound went winding out across the canyon, echoing across the lake and following Kirk who, with a torch of brushwood kindled from the supply he had in the saddle pack, led his horse into the darksome tunnel that thrust under the mountain towards the outside world.

It was a difficult and laborious journey through the tunnel. The small tunnel led into the larger passage at a point close to the crevasse he had passed on his inward journey, and identifying the fateful spot in the wavering half-light, he realised with satisfaction that there was only one real entrance to Lost Canyon – by way of the dried-up watercourse he had followed from the Valley of Little Lost.

It was late in the evening when he finally reached the end of his trek under the mountain, and he made his last camp under the lee of the tunnel cliff, and slept fitfully until dawn.

He was now in that curious state of mind that knew neither excitement nor regret. Everything he did was automatic. It was as though having closed his mind against the possibility of any reactionary decision altering his prearranged plans, every move he made was a mere functioning of nerve and sinew already atuned to the grim task he had to do.

In the same mechanical state of mind, he broke camp and led his horse well down the trail, leaving him tethered while he returned to put into effect the last dramatic part of his plan.

He noticed that no sign of Unwin and his gang could be seen, although he did discern a scattering of hoof marks leading towards the Valley of the Little Lost and guessed thereby that Dark Fury and the herd had harried the unwelcomed visitors all the way down the trail.

The keg of gunpowder was still there, as he expected, and the sight of it stiffened his resolution. He would seal off the canyon forever. Having no exact knowledge of the means of setting off such a charge of explosive, he decided to make as long a fuse trail as was possible,

203

and it took him best of an hour to achieve his purpose. Satisfied at last, he stood within the tunnel listening intently for any sign of movement. His only dread lay in the possibility that maybe Dark Fury had decided to follow him. No sound however did he hear, and he judged it safe to proceed with his plan.

Ten minutes later from a point of safety well away from the mountain, he fired the powder trail, and then took refuge behind an outcrop of rock to await the result.

Time seemed drawn out to some vague resemblance of eternity as he crouched waiting. He could see the powder trail smouldering as the main heat force moved up towards the keg in the tunnel mouth. Then for a very long time, it seemed he could see nothing at all. He waited with his heart intrepid in its beating. Perhaps in his inexperience he had not fired the powder with sufficient accuracy. Maybe he ought to go back and investigate. His body quivered with a sense of shock at the thought. Perhaps then he would find the keg about to explode and . . . .

Kirk closed his eyes, his lips pressed tightly together.

Then his body stiffened, and he lay rigid. He opened his eyes and looked upwards at the mountain. A dull roar came to his ears, a roar like the prolonged rolling of drums, and a cloud of smoke whirled upwards . . . .

Nothing more could he see but that cloud of smoke whirling upwards, acrid and black. What followed seemed scarcely real. The whole mountain became instinct with life, moving perceptibly, then settling down, without even the movement of a boulder . . . just settling down over the cavern that, in the moment of the settling, was a cavern no longer.

An hour later, an eagle came soaring unperturbed over the peak, followed by its mate. Then from some place up amidst the scattering of spruce and cedar came the voice of a mocking bird, calling . . . calling . . . .

It was well into the afternoon when Kirk was met on that downward trail by none other than Washakie himself. The meeting was most casual as if both men were but travellers going from one place to another. The Indian listened patiently to what Kirk had to say and nodded his head gravely.

'You disobeyed orders from Red Cloud; but you done well. You done what Cœur D'Alenes planned to do when black stallion back in canyon.' He nodded his head once again. 'You good white man. You close canyon against evil men who would destroy hoss and take canyon gold. Red Cloud, he be pleased to call you Blood Brother. Come!'

Washakie turned his mustang about and rode off down the trail, leaving Kirk to follow.

Maybe an hour or more passed without a word being uttered between them, then as the westering sun struck the ridge of Grouse Creek Mountain, Washakie halted, and half-turning, pointed upwards.

'See ... up on cliff ... only place where black hoss can look down upon Valley of Little Lost ....'

Kirk stood up in the stirrups to look back.

He uttered a low cry.

He found himself looking up on to the false divide which he had visited from Lost Canyon, and as the glow of the fast westering sun fell full upon it, he could discern a single shape standing between the towering cliffs that marked the ancient height.

Washakie acknowledged his look of enquiry with a smile.

'Dark Fury ... he look down upon Valley of Little Lost to see you make safe journey. He veree great hoss an' know you bin good to him ... not like bad men who come no more to valley ....'

'What happened to them?' Kirk enquired eagerly.

Washakie shrugged his shoulders.

'It no matter now. One thing certain. They come no more to Valley of Little Lost. Dark Fury an' herd scared them bad, an' drove them down trail to lake. Cœur D'Alenes then do rest ....'

He shook his head once again, this time a little reflectively, Kirk thought.

'Valley be a better place now,' the Indian added; and hearing him speak thus, Kirk knew that this was Washakie's last word on the subject.

Then, for the very first time that day, he felt his heart lift a little within him, lift and rejoice; and as he continued to gaze back at the false divide on Grouse Creek Mountain, he saw the afterglow waver, grow red and fade. Still that small shape he knew to be the stallion, Dark Fury, stood in the gap between the uprising horns of the cliffs that marked the divide. For a few seconds longer the horse was visible, then Kirk could see no more the divide, nor the horns of the cliffs, nor the shape....

Lost Canyon, Dark Fury ... everything, save perhaps the Valley of Little Lost, might have been a dream. Nothing more remained. Not even a last flickering glow passed along that mountain ridge where a stallion had stood, patiently watching.

Yet, perhaps, one last sign was vouchsafed to him – or was it only in his ears he heard it – the distant clarion call like a bugle note winding down from above?

Kirk looked to Washakie as if to confirm the sound he thought he could hear.

The Indian regarded him impassively.

Kirk knew then that all he heard was the silence – the silence of a mountain ancient with the years it had known as it looked down upon the Valley of Little Lost and kept guard over the canyon where the last of the great wild horse herds dwelt protected for ever....

HERE ENDS THE HISTORY OF DARK FURY,
WRITTEN AS A TRIBUTE TO
THOSE WHO ASSIST IN THE
PROTECTION OF ALL WILD
LIFE IN THE VAST NATURE
CONSERVANCIES THROUGHOUT
THE WORLD.

More Beaver Books

We hope you have enjoyed this Beaver Book. Here are some of the other titles:

Ghost Horse A dramatic story about a legendary stallion in the American West; by Joseph E. Chipperfield

The Coral Wreck A mysterious scroll with clues which lead to a sunken Spanish treasure ship provide hero Dirk Rogers with exciting and sometimes dangerous adventures in the South Seas; by Frank Crisp

Riding and Schooling A Beaver original. The third book in the Young Riders Guides series by Robert Owen and John Bullock. Illustrated with black and white photographs and line drawings

My Favourite Horse Stories Dorian Williams has chosen fifteen of his favourite stories and poems about horses, by authors such as Tolstoy, Shakespeare and Dick Francis; a collection to delight all animal lovers

The Glass Knife John Tully's gripping and intriguing story about a boy who has been reared to become a human sacrifice. Set in South America before the European discovery of the New World; illustrated by Victor Ambrus

White Fang Jack London's great classic story about the life of a wild wolf dog at the time of the Gold Rush in the Yukon

New Beavers are published every month and if you would like the *Beaver Bulletin* – which gives all the details – please send a large stamped addressed envelope to:

Beaver Bulletin
The Hamlyn Group
Astronaut House
Feltham
Middlesex TW14 9AR

329526